The
Distant Friend

The
Distant Friend

a novel

Claude Roy

Translated by Hugh A. Harter
Introduction by Jack Kolbert

HM

HOLMES & MEIER
New York / London

Published in the United States of America 1990 by
Holmes & Meier Publishers, Inc.
30 Irving Place
New York, NY 10003

Originally published in French under the title *L'ami lointain*,
copyright © Éditions Gallimard, Paris, 1987.

The paper used in this publication meets the requirements of the American
National Standard for Permanence of Paper for Printed Library Materials,
Z39.48-1984.

Library of Congress Cataloging-in-Publication Data

Roy, Claude, 1915–
  [Ami lointain. English]
  The distant friend : a novel / Claude Roy ; translated by Hugh A.
  Harter.
    p. cm.
  Translation of: L'ami lointain.
  ISBN 0-8419-1196-7 (alk. paper)
  I. Title.
PQ2635.09644A4513   1990
843'.914—dc20   90-30540
                                       CIP

Manufactured in the United States of America

Introduction

Jack Kolbert

Critics and historians of twentieth-century French literary life know that Claude Roy's presence has been a most ubiquitous one. His name is encountered just about everywhere: as a novelist, poet, essayist, critic, journalistic reviewer, art critic, travel writer, and biographer. There is virtually no chronicle on contemporary letters in France which does not cite Roy's name several times. Despite this renown in his native country, he is scarcely known in America, where he has not yet received the recognition he clearly merits. One of the reasons for his obscurity in the United States stems from the fact that relatively few of his works have been translated into English. With the publication of *The Distant Friend*, in a sensitive and faithful translation by Hugh A. Harter, English-language readers can begin to appreciate the richness of Claude Roy's fiction.

Born on 28 August 1915 in Paris, with the name of Claude Orland, the author of *The Distant Friend* (*L'ami lointain,* 1987) adopted the pseudonym of Claude Roy early in his literary life. He studied at the Lycée Montaigne in Paris as well as at the Lycée in Angoulême, where he received his baccalaureate degree. At the age of twenty he entered the Sorbonne at the University of Paris. When World War II began, he enlisted in his nation's armed services and was involved in active combat in Lorraine as the result of his role in a major tank battalion. Decorated with the military honor of Croix de Guerre, Roy was captured by the Germans and placed in a military camp outside Metz. The period of incarceration, an exceedingly painful episode in his life, ended abruptly when he successfully escaped and fled to the so-called Free Zone in Southern France.

During his formative years, Roy had been active in the ultra-right-wing, super-patriotic movement of intellectuals, L'Action Francaise. There his closest literary associates were Thierry Maulnier, a well-known critic, and Robert Brasillach, a fairly popular novelist. But the imprisonment in a Nazi military camp and the drama of France's defeat in World War II played a profound part in his intellectual development. Almost without transition, he transformed himself from a right-wing extremist to a card-carrying member of the Communist party, whose members were after all in the vanguard of the Resistance Movement fighting against the forces that occupied his beloved France.

During the rest of the Nazi Occupation of France, Claude Roy fought actively in the Resistance, and his name was closely identified with the underground intellectuals of the period, especially with Aragon, Eluard, and Roger

Vailland. He even worked as a war correspondent between the First French Army and the First American Army.

Following the Liberation of France, Roy continued to champion Communist causes. He took his first trip to the United States in 1949. Two years later he traveled to China and Korea. In 1952 this admirer of the Soviet Union took a trip to that country also. Soon thereafter his wanderlust took him to French North Africa, Czechoslovakia, and Poland. But his enthusiasm for Communist philosophy diminished sharply by 1956, especially when he witnessed the brutality with which the Soviets destroyed the freedom fighters of the Hungarian Revolution. Speaking out stridently against Soviet behavior in Hungary, Roy soon found himself placed in an untenable position among his fellow Communists. The party excommunicated him, an event which he seemed to welcome: he revolted against the abuses of Stalin's orthodox approach to Socialism.

That Roy could undergo such rapid transformations— from one extreme of the political spectrum (L'Action Française) to another (Communism) attests to his intellectual adaptability. Refusing to enslave himself to errors of political judgment, he insisted on total freedom to develop a philosophy of life that conformed with his sense of what was right and wrong. This willingness to change is also evident in his facility with literary styles and methods. It seems as if he can effortlessly write in any kind of genre or style that he chooses.

In 1966 Roy took a second trip to the Soviet Union. He returned even more convinced that Communism was not an appropriate political commitment for him. Since that year, he has devoted himself fully to the life of the pen and has served as a member of the Committee of Readers with the prestigious publishing firm of Gallimard, which has produced most of his works.

As a prelude to a more detailed discussion of *The Distant Friend*, it may be useful to mention several distinctive characteristics of Roy's literary art in general. In the first place, Claude Roy is fundamentally a poet in everything he writes. Having launched his career as a writer of verse, and being under the spell of the leading surrealist poets of our century, Roy readily started to view the universe through the lenses of poetry. Deeply sensitive to natural phenomena—to trees, flowers, blades of grass, streams and rivers—he learned to formulate metaphors and images with impressive vividness and nuanced subtleties. He effortlessly transformed his poetic style into the sentences found in the prose narratives of his novels and short fiction. So it is not surprising that some of the most admirable pages in *The Distant Friend* are richly laden with descriptive passages of sheer poetry. But this poetic prose is more than merely descriptive. Actually, as he deals with the inner soul of his characters—their feelings, memories, and outlooks on life—it is as if he were writing lyrical poetry.

Hugh A. Harter's translation is the kind that Claude Roy deserves. It retains the low-keyed, understated, bittersweet language and tone of the original. Harter, professor emeritus of Ohio Wesleyan University, is especially felicitous in his translations of the poetic passages (for example, the idyllic scene when Stefan and his childhood companion go fishing along a lovely German stream). But he does an equally effective job in his translations of the more brutal scenes (as in the case of the two Nazi thugs who bully the two younger Jewish boys, or in the terrifying scene in Argentina).

The second prominent feature in Roy's art is his ability to look at life and people with unusually keen perception. His "glance" or "look" takes in traits or features in people that normally go unnoticed. Tiny details of behavior, the most delicate feelings, the slightest shift in moods, he describes with variegated shadings and minute observations. Thus the principal characters in *The Distant Friend* are rendered and developed with extraordinary sensitivity.

Another strength in Roy's works, stemming from his love for travel, is his ability to create a variety of settings in powerful detail. Scenes in his works take place not only in his native France but also in many other countries. In *The Distant Friend*, for example, the novelist evokes both Breuil and Moustier, two villages located in the southwestern region of France (probably in the area around Bordeaux or in the region of the Charentes Maritimes), and the greater Buenos Aires region, parts of the northeastern United States, Germany, and of course Paris.

Just as Roy conveys the mood and appearance of geographical places, so does his sharp observation of sociopolitical movements in Hitleristic Germany, post-Peronista Argentina, and in the France before, during, and after World War II serve him well in his efforts to recapture the political upheavals witnessed by the characters in *The Distant Friend*.

Roy is also truly superb in the psychological analyses of his principal characters. His treatment of tensions between brothers (Etienne and Olivier), the situation between a rebellious teenage daughter and her more rational father (Sara and Stefan), the strained rapport between a loyal but burdened son and his dying, elderly mother (Etienne and his mother), and many other human entanglements—all of this is the work of a master of human psychology.

It is, however, when Claude Roy dissects the relationship of two male friends, Etienne, the narrator, and Stefan, his closest friend, that we discern this author's true command of the subject of human psychology. No more perceptive depiction of friendship between two men has been written in French literature since Montaigne's celebrated essay "De l'amitié" in the sixteenth century.

What is the most glaring weakness in the otherwise admirable literary art of Claude Roy? In my view, the problem stems mainly from his incredible literary facility with stylistic machinations of all sorts. Roy is an outstanding *pasticheur,* someone who can place himself inside the skin of the authors he admires most, and who can write pastiches of their work. When he writes poems, he composes verse that is more Aragonesque than that of Louis Aragon. In some of his novelistic works he out-Stendhalizes the author of *The Red and the Black.* When he deals with remembrances of times past, he rivals Marcel Proust. In his poetic evocations of dreamlike provincial landscapes, he emulates *Le Grand Meaulnes* of Alain-Fournier. His extraordinary facility in pastiches and his propensity for imitating those writers he adulates often ends up in a literary style that is flawless in its own right but conceals from us the identity of the real Claude Roy. His texts are sometimes too brilliantly done, too perfect, too filled with a virtuoso talent for adapting himself to the personalities of other writers or adopting the peculiar rhythms of their unique characters. Yet none of these agilities in styles, images, or moods diminishes the attractiveness of Roy's books. Indeed a work like *The Distant Friend* is an eminently readable, even a memorable work of novelistic art. His variety of themes, styles, and artistic stances is immense.

In *The Distant Friend*, Etienne the narrator resembles Claude Roy in many ways. More or less a man of Roy's own generation, he has grown up with his brother Olivier in Breuil, an old manor house in an unidentified southwestern French province, probably near the Bordeaux, Poitier, or Angoulême region. The house is the epitome of a traditional French provincial abode, the kind to which so many people from Paris or one of the other large Franch cities like to escape for their regular holidays. Etienne's father, a taciturn fellow, hardly articulates anything mainly because he cannot compete with the more domineering mother who is so incessantly garrulous. Both parents quite obviously manifest much greater interest in the professional outcome of Olivier, who possesses the kind of drive and high energy level to become a noted university philologist and a productive Parisian scholar, than in their other son, Etienne, a fairly lackluster, passive type who resigns himself to being second best in everything that takes place in the household.

When the father dies, Olivier refuses to interrupt his successful career in order to care for the property and especially to take over the responsibilities of their elderly mother. So Etienne, who bends with the wind unprotestingly, ends up performing these dual tasks. The mother, a heavy burden for Etienne, especially in her last years of illness, dies. The story opens with her death, an event which prompts both Etienne and Olivier to reminisce about vanished days and childhood. Isolated episodes from the past are unearthed from their memory as they browse through old family photograph albums.

Some of these photographs depict Etienne's closest friend, Stefan (or Stephan), a young Jewish friend whose family had been forced to flee Nazi Germany and to move to Moustier, a tiny village not too far from Breuil. The two friends were originally united at the seashore where they spent their vacations, and each becomes the alter ego for the other.

What is most noteworthy in *The Distant Friend* is the fact that such an unusually rich friendship should have blossomed between two young men who were so entirely disparate in temperament, family background, culture, fundamental values, national origin, and above all religion. Etienne symbolizes traditional Catholic, provincial, stable France at its best. Stefan, on the other hand, epitomizes rootlessness, restlessness, and European cosmopolitanism as only Jewish intellectuals forced to wander from land to land could embody.

This relationship is interrupted geographically when

Stefan is forced to depart for the New World in 1939, two days before the outbreak of the Second World War. Unable to emigrate to the United States because of quotas on immigration there, Stefan and his family go instead to Buenos Aires. Between 1939 and 1945, while Etienne spends the Occupation years in a more or less active role in the French Resistance movement (one of the few times when he actually harnessed enough energy to engage himself in a worthwhile cause), Stefan becomes an internationally renowned professor of law. Marrying Nora, an American socialite who moves to Argentina with him, Stefan has an only child, Sara. Occasionally he manages to correspond with Etienne, and the two friends are able, at least occasionally, to communicate with each other and, later, are reunited and separated once again.

The Distant Friend ends with an epilogue-like chapter in which Etienne, with bittersweet sadness, recalls the many beautiful moments shared by the two men in the past. This long relationship has, in essence, been the most precious part of the narrator's existence; in fact, it is the one force that has given meaning to his entire life. And so Etienne, who in the past had rarely been able to muster enough energy to create anything of real significance, will recapture the beauty of his friendship with Stefan by composing a book for posterity. *The Distant Friend* thus becomes the one indelible monument exalting their relationship.

Several major intersecting themes constitute the opaque texture of the novel, and, of the most important ones, the first that comes to mind is that of history itself. *The Distant Friend*, in Roy's subtle, indirect, and understated literary style, is not only the story of a beautiful friendship; it is also the narration of an important and tragic chapter in world history. We witness the sad history of the Jewish people, from the rise of Hitleristic anti-Semitism in Nazi Germany to the poisons of another totalitarian regime in post-Peronista Argentina. This history is sensitively elaborated through the suffering of one Jewish family, that of the Steins (Stefan's family name), as they are forced to abandon their family home in Germany—where Stefan's father had been an internationally acclaimed ornithologist—then ending up in France, where the scientific community is slow to accept and to support Dr. Stein's place within the family of scientists, and finally in Argentina where the late Dr. Stein's son Stefan suffers death at the hands of his captors.

That the Catholic Claude Roy should have demonstrated such an uncanny understanding of the psychology of being a Jew is another example of his intellectual pliancy. Some of the most realistic pages in Roy's novel are those in which the author analyzes tensions arising from the relationships between the assimilated Germanic family of Stefan Stein and their unassimilated cousins in Paris who seek to provide them with hospitality when they arrive in the French capital. But the novelist aptly demonstrates how, in the wake of the Nazi threat, all factions of Judaism unite and of course ultimately suffer the same grim fate of destruction in the Holocaust.

Roy stresses the rapport between anti-Semitism and the

deterioration of law in certain states. He describes how Stefan observed "the progressive and simultaneous extinction of the law and the state, as both were to become equally useless." And when the latter set out for Argentina, he "set out for a country where law and rights were no more than words." So Roy analyzes the relationship between law and rights, on the one hand, with racial-ethnic-religious discrimination, on the other. A powerful and grim element in Roy's novel is the fact that decades following the destruction of Nazism, anti-Semitism and its concomitant socio-psychological diseases remain alive and well around the world, especially in countries with unstable social and political foundations, e.g., Argentina. Like the pessimistic philosopher, Martin, in *Candide* by Voltaire, an author whom Claude Roy admired, he stated that "The history of a great nation is a web of petty atrocities, score settlings disguised as battles, of fights between cowherds cutting one another open. . . . Everything is a mess—the piping, the plumbing, the surfacing of the streets, the conscience of those who do the governing, and the spine of those who are governed."

Roy's depiction of anti-Semitism is thus expanded into the study of state crimes, questions of law and order, radicalism vs. conservatism, extremism vs. moderation, left vs. right. In effect, some of the most eloquent pages are devoted to political dialogue, especially between Stefan (the rational moderate) and his daughter Sara (a more zealously committed revolutionary) and between Stefan and Etienne.

If the Frenchman represents inaction and conservatism,

his cosmopolitan Jewish friend stands for openness to change, willingness to consider the many political and social options available to the human race, and a readiness to adopt positions according to the vagaries of an ever-shifting historical situation. In this respect, one senses that Stefan more truly reflects the actual situation of Claude Roy himself, who, as we have seen, made the shift from a right-wing affiliation to Communist party membership. And precisely because the author himself knew the meaning of right- and left-wing politics, he could portray the two with utter authenticity. Roy is especially effective as he describes the dilemma experienced by Etienne, who works within the network of the Resistance movement during the Occupation, a network within which there were both strong tendencies toward super-patriotism in the manner of de Gaulle and also socialist sympathies for Soviet-styled movements, with both conflicting forces working to subvert the strength of the occupying German forces.

Of all of the political tensions treated in *The Distant Friend*, however, none is more dramatic than the one involved in the anti-Jewish fervor that swept Nazi Germany. The whole tension, in all of its ugliness, is masterfully recaptured by Roy in the most pivotal episode of the entire novel: the idyllic fishing scene when Stefan and a boyhood friend find themselves brutally humiliated—both physically and psychologically—by two somewhat older Nazi thugs, both of whom resemble in their physical appearance, Laurel and Hardy. Years later, in Argentina, Stefan Stein is arrested by Argentine ruffians and mysteriously vanishes in the maelstrom of political upheaval. Investigation after investigation by the "authorities" in Argentina fails to come up with plausible explanations for this disappearance until, thanks to an inadvertent leak, Etienne learns to his horror that his alter ego had been brutalized and tortured—and his two interrogators resemble Laurel and Hardy. History repeats itself.

There is another compelling theme here: the contrast between roots and rootlessness. Roy reflects the ongoing debate in France between those who accentuate the importance of having family roots that are deeply embedded in the soil of their provincial origins and those who believe that the strength of French culture stems from the nation's capacity to absorb people from the most diverse backgrounds. This debate seemed to have once reached its apogee during the polemic between two of the writers Claude Roy admired fervently: André Gide and Maurice Barrès. Etienne symbolizes the national French character of being deeply rooted in the soil of nation, family, and tradition. Most of his ancestors were either priests or soldiers. For his part, Stefan Stein stands for nomadism and extreme rootlessness. His is a nomadism that has been forced upon his family. That the destinies of two such unlike persons should have become so inextricably intertwined is one of the central facts of the novel, all of which leads us to the principal theme of *The Distant Friend:* that of friendship.

The friendship between Etienne and Stefan is a compelling example of how two seemingly incompatible personalities can merge, through some accident of human destiny, and out of this union there emerges a total harmony. Through a friend one may find self-fulfillment and self-understanding. Etienne had never comprehended his own passive nature nor had he appreciated the extent to which his parents preferred his brother Olivier to him until the outside observer, Stefan, analyzed his true character for him. Similarly, through Etienne's eyes Stefan realized his own strengths and virtues. Roy, speaking through his protagonist Etienne, defines friendship like this: "Friendship's passion, that joyous movement of the spirit and the blood that animated me, the desire to talk with Stefan, to be with him and to verify myself through him, drove me to acts which I would have thought myself incapable of doing." And when Olivier points out to Etienne that "He [Stefan] was in one world, and you in the other," the French friend realized that the disparity of their two worlds was really illusory. Deep down in their souls both friends shared common values and mutual respect. Etienne admits that "His world seemed to me to be the real world, the world of life." The "world of life" really signified an existence of accomplishments, dreams fulfilled, travel, suffering, anguish, anxiety, the joy of husbandhood and fatherhood. And Etienne lived this kind of life only vicariously, through the trials and triumphs of his best, if not only, true friend. Above all, he experienced, thanks to Stefan's attentiveness, something that neither his parents nor his brother allowed him to sense even once during his entire lifetime: "I had the feeling that I was *important* to someone." Their friendship was no short-lived adventure; it lasted forty-eight years. A concomitant theme, in fact, is that of two comrades who age together, who observe from decade to decade the physical transformations in each other. This aging together contributes much to the beauty of Claude Roy's presentation of the overall theme of friendship.

Recounted entirely in the first person by the narrator, the novel leaps back and forth chronologically in stream-of-consciousness fashion. Past blends into present, and present into past. The one tense lacking here is future. As the novel concludes, the only thing we can be certain of is the continuity of the present into the future. For we are left in suspension. Tiny details, minute events shift the narrator's recapitulation of one moment in his past to another one that is further in the recesses of time. The most effective device for shifting time is that of the family photograph album, a device that opens up all sorts of memories for the protagonists. As Etienne tries to recall someone in an old picture he states: "But on examining it, like all other theological inventions, it surely contains a small kernel of truth in a symbolic way. Those we can still name are retained by that fragile thread, not of life, because they obviously no longer enjoy it, but they are held for an instant in our memories suspended at the edge of the abyss of time where oblivion will swallow up their name."

Let us remember that at the time of the composition of *The Distant Friend*, the author was already in the autumnal stage of his life. In the midst of his seventh decade he understandably was prone to reminisce, to reflect upon the meaning of life and literature. In its own special fashion, this novel is the story about a budding writer who sets out to write a story. Etienne the narrator thus writes a novel that will transform an otherwise beautiful human relationship seemingly doomed to disappear into a bittersweet work of literary art that through the alchemy of words and metaphors will outlive Stefan and himself. Here is how Etienne (Claude Roy) expresses his idea of literature: "If I were to write the novel whose author I have been dreaming of being since adolescence, it would begin here, in the way that all true novels end, when the ship of life is sinking or the waterway has already disappeared, destiny already sealed and set and the game lost. . . . But I am no doubt the only one today who has the impression of living an epilogue, of being the end of something."

In Simone Signoret's autobiography, *La Nostalgie n'est plus ce qu'elle était* (1970), which appeared in an English translation eight years later (*Nostalgia Isn't What It Used to Be*), the French actress parenthetically tells her readers that she used to frequent cafés in Paris with her close friend, the singer Yves Montand, in order to listen to the "Russian Frank Sinatra" (Bernès) sing a hauntingly beautiful song entitled "L'ami lointain." (We know from Signoret's work that both she and Montand were close friends of Claude Roy.) It is thus entirely possible, if not probable, that he was inspired by this song when he named what may well be his finest novel.

On Claude Roy's Other Writings

Claude Roy's literary output is both impressive and vast. It spills over into virtually every literary genre. Here is only a partial panorama of the titles he produced over the years.

In the arena of pure poetry Roy has written a number of collections of verse, most of which manifest his profound interest in surrealism. His verse is especially reminiscent of the writings of Apollinaire, Jules Supervielle, Paul Eluard, and Louis Aragon, all leaders in contemporary French poetry. A few of Roy's collections include: *Claire comme le jour* (1943), *Le Bestiaire des amants* (1946), *Le Poète mineur* (1949), *Elégie des lieux communs* (1952; this work includes a portrait of Roy by Picasso), *Le Parfait Amour* (1952), and *Un seul poème* (1954). Among his assorted novels and short narrative prose we ought to include *La Nuit est le manteau des pauvres* (originally issued in 1948 and redone in 1968), *A tort ou à raison* (1955), *Le Soleil sur la terre* (1956), *Le Malheur d'aimer* (1958), *Léone et les siens* (1963), and *La Dérobée* (1968). Many of these novels show the influence of Stendhal, Giraudoux and Alain-Fournier.

The largest group of Roy's works falls under the rubric of literary criticism and essays, and some of these titles were best-sellers in his native France. During the Nazi Occupation he published his first critical work, *L'Enfance de l'art* (1942), followed by *Suite Française* (1943), *Les Yeux ouverts dans Paris insurgé* (1944), and *Aragon* (1945). After the Liberation he devoted himself to a number of critical volumes on French classicism, painting, and contemporary authors, all of which he categorized under the general heading of *Descriptions critiques* (5 volumes, published between 1949 and 1960). Roy was especially perspicacious in his critical analyses of authors he admired the most: for example: *Lire Marivaux* (1947), *Stendhal par lui-même*

(1957), *Jules Supervielle* (1964). His art criticism is most impressive, and among twentieth-century writers he stands out as one of the most astute commentators on the visual arts, especially when dealing with artists whose work he admired most or whom he knew from his personal contacts with them. Here is but a partial sampling of Roy's art criticism: *Maillol* (1947), *Goya* (1952), *Picasso* (1954), *Jean Lurçat* (1956), *Modigliani* (1958), and *Paul Klée* (1960). Some of his collections of critical essays are essentially chronicles of travel literature based on his own personal peregrenations: e.g., *Clefs pour l'Amérique* (1947), *Premières Clefs pour la Chine* (1950), *Clefs pour la Chine* (1953), *La Chine dans un miroir* (1953), and *Le Journal des voyages* (1960).

Among the most curious of the miscellaneous titles published by the author of *L'ami lointain* are some delightful children's books; especially noteworthy are *La Famille quatre cents coups* (1954) and *Farandoles et Fariboles* (1957). We notice that the decades of the fifties and sixties were the most fertile years for Claude Roy. During the seventies he became more retrospective in his approach to literary problems and began to compose autobiographical books. Noteworthy are three monumental volumes on his life entitled *Moi, je* (1969), *Nous* (1972), and *Somme toute* (1976). During the most recent times his other works have assumed a more introspective character. From his earliest stance as an *auteur engagé*, that is, a writer who had committed himself to the defense of political and social causes, Roy now seems much more interested in producing works in which he searches for moments long since past. His art seems to be developing in the mode of Marcel Proust. The search for self-understanding and for sources for his current feelings prevails increasingly in his prose, and memory plays an all-pervasive role in his latest works.

The
Distant Friend

· 1 ·

At Pique-Chidouille Cemetery, the jack-of-all-trades for the dead said to me: "There is still space for two of you, Monsieur Etienne. There are two vaults free in the crypt. Too bad you're not married." I looked at the two unmarked headstones. I thought of the checkrooms in railway stations. I could leave my baggage at the cemetery checkroom. My baggage isn't heavy, despite the years. It is made up of all the things I haven't done. I never married. I've had no children. I wanted to see something of the world, to travel. I stayed here. I wanted to write. It was Stefan who published. It was my brother who was given the freedom to work on the thesis he's talked about turning into a book for years. His "Treatise on Textology" which, he says in a somewhat threatening tone, "will show something new." As for me, I'm afraid I have nothing new to contribute. I would like to understand two or three things about life, to find one or two answers. Sometimes I think I've caught a glimpse of them. Now I know they've escaped me. I have no need of a cubicle in a checkroom. I'd have little to leave there.

The priest stationed himself in front of the grave pit with his holy water and his sprinkler, and motioned me to go with Olivier to the end of the line to receive condolences. The accompanying kisses often leave the mourner's cheeks moist. When it's someone we really love, tears of sympathy dim our eyes.

Olivier said to me last night, "One must have the terrible courage to look truth straight in the eye." My brother never lacked the "terrible courage." I asked, "What truth?" "For you it's a deliverance." I did not reply. I have had the *terrible courage* in question for the three days since Mother finally died. I don't think that any of the people who made the trip, the neighbors who came to pay the customary respects, to "bow" before the corpse—my brother, Julie, and even Vincent himself, yes, not a single one who did not say: "It's a deliverance for her," or the equivalent. (Did she suffer a lot? Now she's no longer suffering . . .) But no one until Olivier had spoken of my own deliverance. I had thought about it, however, with a bit of shame and also with irony. Now, as one says, I have been "freed from my burden." I am free, like the prisoner to whom one announces that the judicial error has finally been recognized, that he is innocent and will be freed after twenty years in prison. But it's a little late: he is given the news in his bed at the main hospital, where the doctors have just made a diagnosis of the beginnings of multiple sclerosis, an irreversible illness.

As I left the cemetery, I passed by the tomb of Stefan's father. "Ernst Friedrich Stein, 1870–1939." I saw at a glance that it is well kept up, as per my instructions. That's one of the obligations I have taken on for Stefan. It was in August of 1939, the evening before the Steins got their visa. Not the one they had hoped for, the United States, but its ersatz, Argentina. They were getting their luggage ready. The Professor must have made a mistake in the departure. Instead of going to South America, he died very suddenly. A heart attack. In life as in death, he looked like an aged bird. Keepers of wine cellars often have noses like a fine bottle, and pork-butchers, snouts like a pig's. Ornithologists have faces and forms of birds. When he learned that his exile was to be Argentina, Professor Stein was delighted, despite the disappointment: "I have always wanted to clarify the system of reproduction of the spinning shrike with yellow eyebrows and to verify on the spot if what Curry-Lindhall says about the migration of the black anhinga is really exact." The Professor was buried so fast—in order for Stefan and his mother to catch their plane—that Stefan had no time to cry.

I sent Stefan a telegram. He called Mother "my French mother." I haven't had any news of him for a long time now.

Burials do not keep people from getting out sheets and tableware. Just the contrary. When I got back home from the station where I had driven my brother, I found Marie and her niece busy putting the house in order. They had already finished cleaning Mother's room and had spirited away the paraphernalia of illness and the accessories of death—bedpan, undersheet, hypodermic needles, medicines, the holy water font and the boxwood. Since it's Wednesday and there is no school today, Marie has mobilized her grandson. He is washing dishes in the scullery next

3

to the kitchen with an unnerving din of plates colliding with one another. On the floor of the linen-room, there is a pile of sheets that were taken from the beds of Olivier, Julie, and Vincent. Yvonne is vacuuming my den, something that had not been done for quite a while because the noise annoyed my mother. She communicated this to us by a series of muffled growls that we had learned to interpret. An approbatory soughing expressed pleasure, while a sort of supplicant growling signified hunger or thirst, and a smothered cry meant "no." We could understand two or three other messages that were incomprehensible to outsiders.

If I were to write the novel whose author I have been dreaming of being since adolescence, it would begin here, in the way that all true novels end, when the ship of life is sinking or the waterway has already appeared, destiny already sealed and set and the game lost, at the moment when Fréderic Moreau tells us that the best moment of his life was the faroff day when he and a friend had planned to go to a brothel and then beat a retreat when they got to the door; when Stendhal finds that Julien Sorel's head was never as *poetic* as when it was about to fall; when Pierre, at the end of *War and Peace,* as he examines the papers of his late wife, perceives that he no longer has any feeling for her whatsoever. But I am no doubt the only one today who has the impression of living an epilogue, of being at the end of something. Olivier has gone back to Paris, and he doesn't seem to think that there will be any end to the steps that he climbs one by one, urged on by his wife, in what is called a "fine career." Elizabeth had been "ailing" and could not come to the burial. "Ailing" was the word that Olivier had used, the one that is utilized in modest terms to avoid talking about an illness, knowing full well that no one believes it. Elizabeth always found Breuil "grim."

She came less and less frequently. We have seen Elizabeth only once since Mother became paralyzed. That stay had been so painful for her that she preferred to be "ailing" far away, in Paris, and never again to be witness to the suffering of others. As for Vincent, he is not a member of the family except for common memories, through the heart. He came as a friend. Knowing him as I do, I think he must have been happy to be near me in those sad moments, and then to leave to go back to those business affairs of his that amuse him so that you never have the impression that Vincent has a business, but that he's only playing games. . . . Julie, his sister . . . But that is another story.

Faced with the agitation of getting the house in order, with the windows open to get rid of the miasmas of the last few days, the noise of the dishes and the vacuum cleaner, and the oppressiveness that I still felt, after nights and days that we had just lived through side by side with death—I decided to get out a bit. I wanted to avoid going through the farm or the vineyards where Mathieu and Maurice had taken up their work again. I didn't feel like talking, like playing the role of "Monsieur Etienne," that person they had known since he was so small, for whose pain they felt compassion, even though in a sense that had been (and here we have that fateful word again) a *deliverance* for Poor Madame. I didn't feel like talking about work either, or discussing with Mathieu the height of the vines or the labors and sowings of autumn, or the upkeep of the property. I had no wish to *talk* with anyone whatsoever.

There was a fine cool November sun in the sky. I put on my old fur-lined jacket, mounted my bike and rode as far as the forest, going by way of the lime-kiln. I hid my bike in the bushes and set off down the forest path. This fine prolonged summer weather obviously could not last. It was relaxing to look with attention at the details of the autumn leaves under the sun that filters through the branches. There is yellow striated with the green of the silver birch, and the golden leaves of the beech that have the effect of the gold masks at the Bogotá museum that were on the postcard that Vincent sent me from there. The leaves of the Austrian oak are mauve yellow. The forest displays a sampling of reds, the carmine of the mountain ash, the oxblood of the cronel tree, the red—like dawn-coming-up-with-rosy-fingers—of the blackberry bushes. The forest smells fresh and good, that odor of fermentation and of the serene putrefaction of leaves that have already fallen and of the autumn humus, that odor that is from the only death that leaves no stench, that vegetable death that links up with life, that death in which the decomposition is already a rebirth, and in which life does not cease to edge its way into the chinks of its own defeat. Some strange thoughts come to my mind, there in that shining forest. I tell myself that Mother is beginning to decompose in the niche of the family vault.

But already a large part of the leaves at the top of the trees where they are less protected have taken on the colors of dull mahogany and drab brown. They are beginning to shrivel up. The first gust of wind or cold spell will brutally strip the branches bare. There was a hedgehog at the edge of the woods on the other side of the metal trellis. It was stupidly and frantically trying to get through, no doubt to take refuge in the forest. It looked at me without even thinking of curling up in a ball. Perhaps it did not know that men are malevolent. They run over hedgehogs with their cars. It did not know that gypsies steam-cook hedgehogs in clay casseroles and eat them. I picked up the little beast as gently as I could. Its quills bristled in my hands, and it closed its eyes to be less afraid, and I put it on the other side of the trellis by the trees, which seemed to be where it wanted to go. It would go off to find a hiding place to hibernate in peace. I wish someone would pick me up in his hands, carry me gently to Breuil and tuck me in to sleep throughout the winter in a hole in the hedge, covered with dead leaves and twigs, invisible to the world and above all to myself.

The hedgehog went off into a thicket, rustling the leaves and grass. I thought again about the experiments of Professor Dimelow on the gastronomic preferences of hedgehogs that I had discovered in the *Treatise on Animal Ethology* of Tinbergen. What nourishes hedgehogs (in order) is canned salmon, chicken, corned beef, poached egg yolk, and then frogs, slugs, snails, earthworms, and finally rotting meat. Mother used to say that the poor do not have the same needs, and therefore not the same tastes, as we do. That way she justified buying cheap cuts of meat for the servants and good cuts for the "masters." But the scientific experiments on the hedgehogs seem to me to prove that the poor have exactly the same tastes that the rich do. Only they don't have the same means to satisfy them.

I walked as far as the charcoal burners' old cabin which now is no more than a ruin, just as the wooden platform installed on the great oak at the crossroads of Vergnes is in ruins. The log stairs that lead up to it are rotting. During summer vacations before the war, the cabin was one of our meeting places. Stefan and I would discuss philosophy and the meaning of history there. There used to be a stuffed long-eared owl in the cabin that stuck up his big dog ears. We baptized him Bourbaki. He would look at us with his lusterless round glass eyes. Were those eyes lusterless because the light of day blinds nocturnal creatures, or was it because of inclemency? Bourbaki is still there. His ochre and dark-brown plumage has been so eaten by moths and gnawed by mice that the naturalist's stuffing is bursting out like some old armchair that indiscriminately spits out its hair and its canvas as it falls apart. Bourbaki surely has aged. I suppose I haven't grown any younger either.

I distractedly caressed Bourbaki's bald head as I thought of the conversation that I had had the night before with my brother. Julie had gone to Marsac to buy an undershirt for old Marie's grandson. Vincent had borrowed my binoculars to go to the bottom of the garden to observe some birds. Olivier and I were in the library. He was looking at some books. He leafed through one of them and said as he replaced it on the shelf, "Actually you pretty much play the role of Uncle Vanya in the family." As I have rarely been to the theater, and for good reason, and since I haven't read

8

Uncle Vanya in twenty or thirty years, if indeed I ever did read it, I answered nothing. "In fact Chekhov is a writer who's a bit overrated," Olivier went on. "There are a lot of words in his sentences, and a lot of 'sentiment' in his words." Olivier pronounced "sentiment" with a movement of disdain in his lower lip.

Last night before I went to bed, I went to get a volume of Chekhov's plays in the library. I read *Uncle Vanya*. The analogy between him and me is less evident than my brother indicated. It's true that after Father's death, I stayed on in Breuil to take care of the property, and of Mother, but I didn't send any money to Olivier. He didn't need any. His career is brilliant enough. He did not suggest we sell Breuil. I didn't shoot him with a revolver, but what hurt me was the objective and detached tone my brother used when he told me I played a role rather like Vanya's. It suggested that he thought he was playing the role of Serebriakov, the brother-in-law as cold as a cold fish who was also a professor as brilliant in Moscow as my brother is in Paris. Of course, Olivier has a great intellect, but he does not always avoid acting the entomologist or zoologist when he has an audience. When you're with him, you sometimes feel like a frog being dissected by a methodical scientist. But that is undoubtedly the price that must be paid when you are dedicated to pure thought—like my brother.

When I got back to Breuil, the women had finished their cleaning. Dingo and Dina welcomed me as if they had lost me for a couple of weeks. The dogs must have understood that from then on I would be alone with them and old Marie in this house that suddenly looked to me like a suit that had been cut too large. My place was set, by itself, in the dining room. I had the impression of its being so for the first time. The last few days, my brother, Julie and Vincent had been at the table with me, but I recalled that I have been at the table alone for many years, ever since Mother's attack. I leaned the newspaper against the carafe of wine from our vineyards and read *Le Monde* and the *Sud-Ouest*, above all the latter with its local news, as I was eating. In the *Sud-Ouest* you learn all the births, marriages, deaths, and that Messieurs Babaud and de Goulet have not paid the debts of Clementine Babaud, née Cassaguet. And also the newspaper serves as a rampart protecting me from my housekeeper's tendency to chatter, the sign that I am engrossed in my reading and am not listening to her. Which does not always keep Marie from unwinding her wordmill, but spares me from having to answer. Once the meal is over, I drink my coffee (decaffeinated coffee ever since my heart acted up), then I go to have a nap upstairs. Afterward I join the men in the fields to see just where we are. In November, the days quickly grow shorter. When night falls, I go up to my library. Tonight I took all the books off the table, all the magazines and papers that had covered it, and I got out some blank paper from the left-hand drawer. It has been there for such a long time without anybody touching it that it has turned a bit yellow. When I used to talk with Mother after her attack, her responses were rudimentary. I was satisfied. Tonight I am writing. In order to speak. To whom? No doubt, just to myself. I certainly have become a very mediocre conversationalist. It's a bit humid and chilly. I'm going to ask Marie to light a good fire in the fireplace.

·2·

During these past months, our old Marie helped the nurse who came every morning to lift, prop up, and install the paralytic in her pillows so that Mother would feel more or less all right. I would place a sort of lectern on her bed table, and I would bring in two or three illustrated books or albums of our family for her to choose from. I would put my finger on them one by one, and when she had let out a sort of groan whose affirmative nuance we had learned to distinguish as meaning "Yes" or "That's it" or "Fine" I would install the volume on the stand and begin to turn the pages for her. Ever since her attack when it became a question of feeding her, giving her something to drink, showing her pictures or photographs or helping in the most elementary movements, her needs, her toilette, the difficulty was to find the right rhythm, to feel and to guess if she had had the time to swallow the spoonful of cereal or to drink the two swallows of water and to look after her self-sufficiency, and were faced with her bad temper because "it took too long a time" with the things we were showing her. I tried to remember if in his *Inferno*

11

Dante had described that torment, that torture of a being who cannot make any movement and who depends for everything on the good will and natural tempo of others. Even those people we call "in good health" have trouble putting up with the slowness or the brusqueness of others. A person who enunciates slowly or who constantly repeats things a second time gets on other people's nerves. The person who struggles with the keys on his ring before he can open the lock exasperates everyone. I don't know who it was who made the following accurate and rare observation: "Evil is the rhythm of others." In the situation in which her paralysis had imprisoned her, Mother had no defense against that particular *evil*. Even when we tried to do something helpful for her, when we overcame the inevitable impatience that sometimes silently disturbs people who take care of the sick, even while we would keep our guilty sense of irritation under control when faced with the immured soul's difficulty in expressing herself, the aged lady remained dependent upon us. She must have resented it every second as an *evil*. There may only be a single dependence that is not a constant anguish, and that's the nursing child holding onto a breast or a baby bottle, if the mother is truly maternal, or one other as well no doubt, that of moments of love that are fully shared. I imagine that in the case of two lovers those moments must abolish all sense, not of dependence (which probably continues to subsist unobtrusively), but the feeling of being in its power.

I would propose several things to Mother, reproductions of paintings, a book on some faraway country or about animals, or else the family photo albums. Nine times out of

12

ten, it was the photographs of the family she would choose, with the breathless short grunt that was her way of expressing her wish. I knew that what she really liked was to go way back to the photos of her own childhood and then to return very slowly, with frequent stops, to the recent past. She tired less quickly with those than with the paintings or the books of photos of foreign countries because she did not look at those pictures from the outside; after all, it was the thread of her own life that she was stitching together again. I had taken the precaution of removing from the last album the latest photographs taken in the garden during Easter vacation, just before the attack that struck Mother down. They showed us having tea under the big lime tree at the end of the terrace. Mother was knitting, my brother Olivier and his wife were talking with her, their little boy was buttering a piece of bread, and Blackie the dog was sniffing attentively around the child in hopes of getting a mouthful for himself. I was reading *Le Monde* in a rattan armchair. The spring sunshine was inching its long fingers of light through the foliage and the flowers of the lime tree. A hundred little lights spangled the faces and bodies like confetti of limpidity scattered by the sun. The first time I turned the pages of that album for Mother, when I got to those images of that afternoon in May, her eyes filled with tears. I understood that the sudden resurgence of that happy moment is beneficial only when the person remembering is still happy. In unhappiness, it is neither a consolation nor a refuge but the burning sensation of regret without hope.

My mother was quite an attractive young woman, and surely coquettish for a provincial village girl, to judge from the changes of coiffures that follow one after another in the photos: a chignon so tightly drawn back it resembles the top of a brioche dominating the tresses held together like a gardener's, then the locks in spirals carefully arranged like shells over the ears for her twentieth birthday. Later on there was a trip to Paris, with a visit to the Museum of Decorative Arts where she wore a cloche and a skirt so short it must have made grandmothers lift their eyebrows. And soon after, the appearance in Breuil of a young agronomist who was assigned there for a stay of three months, and who did not know he was going to live there until his departure for the war in 1939–1940—and until his death, my father.

The moment when Mother showed the most interest, in her muffled and hoarse manner, and perhaps with modest pleasure, was with successive births of the children. Mine first, in diapers on Mother's lap, then my first short trousers, the wheelbarrow I pushed in the garden, and finally the sailor suit for my first communion. The typical sailor suit disappeared from children's lives a long time ago, probably since the disappointment France had to face with her navy, Mers-el-Kabir, the scuttling of the fleet at Toulon, and the politico-naval maneuverings of Admiral Darlan which must have left bad maritime memories in the French subconscious. A year later, my brother Olivier appeared.

The most numerous photos of that period were taken in the best season, in the summertime in the garden. There we had put up a kind of trapper's tent made out of old awnings. Fearlessly, without a twinge in the muscles of my face, I descended an unpassable river infested with hostile

14

redskins on a long plank I'd placed on the grass and that became the canoe of an advance group of prairie settlers. Up front, Olivier paddled with me. Meanwhile, our passenger Julie screamed as the Comanches attacked us and riddled us with arrows from the top of a mountain pass.

Every year in the month of August we went back to the rented villa by the beach of La Conche at Saint-Méjean-sur-Mer. There were few vacation photos of Father because he only came to get us settled in at Saint-Méjean and then went back to Breuil to take care of the summer work. He showed up on the beach only on Saturdays, very late, then left again for Breuil on Sunday evening. Mother kept very busy, despite help from Yvonne, the niece of old Marie from Breuil, whom we brought with us to Saint-Méjean. She helped Mother and took swimming lessons in the afternoon. She was clearly behind the rest of us because I was already plunging into the brink without buoy or belt while Yvonne was still tied up in a lifejacket and glued to an old tire and repeatedly was swallowing mouthfuls.

The world of vacation photographs is similar to those that memory refashions with a selective optimism. It is a world where it has never rained and the sky has never clouded over, a world of perpetual sun in the brilliant light that provides the amateur photographer with the assurance that the picture will turn out well. You could have said that the weather was perpetually fine on the sands of La Conche in the years before the war. Mother, Aunt Geneviève, and their friends Madame Lhoumeau and Madame Paillard sit enthroned under a tent with orange and yellow stripes, installed on folding chairs and surrounded by sacks from which they pulled balls of wool for the perpetual knitting, the food for the children, the thermos bottle and the appurtenances of seaside comfort that transformed each departure into a major expedition. Only the children stayed in bathing suits all day, wearing short-sleeved shirts and canvas hats to avoid getting sunburned—which was not always the case, and fevers this set off kept us confined to bed in the dark while those happy few who had been spared, more sensible than we, were out swimming, gathering seashells, and constructing fortresses in the sand that the rising tide would soon conquer. The mothers, who seemed to us already old (I realize today that they were still quite young women and that nowadays they would probably spend the whole day bathing in the sun), donned their one-piece black bathing costumes, very prim, only to go into the water. Aunt Geneviève, who was the oldest of the group and who complained of all sorts of ailments, "guarded" the encampment while her friends went swimming. The mothers' ceremonial for bathing began with the closing of the canvas doors of the family tent while the ladies were changing. When the doors reopened, they surged forth like the Three Graces of an Italian Renaissance painting, a bit more in the likeness of Juno than of Venus. They moved with dignity toward the water, instructing Aunt Geneviève and the biggest child (that was me) to look after the little ones. It took lengthy negotiations carried out by the shivering feet of the mothers, prudently testing the temperature of the water, it took four or five sallies toward the waves, sallies that were brought to outright halts by sudden retreats, before we could finally perceive their bathing bonnets afloat, almost immobile, on the surface of the water like rubber balloons, while their arms slowly configured a breaststroke without any athletic pretensions, all at a good distance from waves of any size.

I must have been fifteen years old when the Lhoumeau family that I had known from my school began to come, like us, to spend the summer at Saint-Méjean. Vincent was one grade ahead of me at the Collège de Trassac. He and his sister lived in a small neighboring town where Monsieur Lhoumeau was director of a branch of the Crédit Lyonnais bank. The Lhoumeaus were real city people. Vincent and Julie had passed almost all of their childhood in the big cities of the southwest, including Toulouse and Bordeaux. It was because of the bad health of Madame Lhoumeau's aging mother, who was our neighbor, that Monsieur Lhoumeau was able to have himself named to a position which, for any other reasons or less good family reasons, would have looked like a demotion. Vincent was only a year older than I, but we admired him with something like consternation. He smoked High Life cigarettes of light Orient tobacco, and he seemed to "know" women. He organized poker parties in study hall and played jazz piano. In those days, segregation of the sexes still reigned in the school system. At the girls' collège, Julie Lhoumeau had a reputation as suggestive of fire and brimstone as that of her brother at the boys' collège. They said she wore lipstick and makeup for parties organized during the absence of their parents when the latter went to stay overnight at old Madame Lhoumeau's house to take care of her during one of her illnesses. Vincent and Julie, heartless grandchildren,

17

took advantage of the absence to throw a party. It was also said that Julie smoked one cigarette after another in those parties without even trying to hide it. At school, they said, she couldn't hold her tongue and spoke back to the principal, the awesome Mademoiselle Réau. They asserted also that . . . But what didn't they say? They went so far as to whisper that Julie had been seen being kissed in an automobile, not by a boy (which would have been *shocking enough*) but by a *man,* the internist who was replacing Doctor Coutrat during his vacation. Julie, however, didn't look like a *femme fatale.* In the photos, you can see flickering a laughing will-o'-the-wisp, her eyes wrinkled with malice, her pale blond hair pulled back in a ponytail with an elastic band and burned tanner than was sensible because she was constantly getting herself into games with the boys.

Vincent and Julie dazzled me because they were the provincial version of rebelliousness and a bohemian life style. Vincent played old pieces on the piano, out-of-style things by Jack Hylton that he interspersed with the latest swing whose orthodox definitions were done by Hugues Panassié in *Jazz Hot.* He knew how to talk to girls. He knew recipes for cocktails that he prepared himself in a shaker just like the 20s. During their parties, he served us a *rosé* or a *banana-martini,* his own recipe that was creamy and treacherous. He had his suits custom-made by the best tailor in Poitiers. Julie wore clothes that looked like the latest in chic to us, but that I learned later on belonged to a period that was already a bit out of style. She played the role of the 1928 flapper, of the young, free and easy *femme fatale* in old Clara Bow films. She danced, smoked and flirted in the style of the year of the Exposition of Decorative Arts, and even if she dressed like the models in the recent photos of the women's fashion magazines, her mannerisms and her tastes were slightly off-target. In 1935, she lived like a character out of 1925. I admired her joking insolence just as I feared my brother and his quiet condescension.

It was the beach at Saint-Méjean that brought us together with the Lhoumeaus. My parents would not have maintained relations with them on their own at either Breuil or Trassac, first of all because my father was not a client of the bank of the Crédit Lyonnais, but did business at the Société Générale; secondly because Vincent was one grade ahead of me; and above all, above all, because although the Lhoumeau children did not exactly have what might be called a *bad reputation*, they came close to it. In any case they were not like other children, they were nonconformist. Even if they did not quite represent evil or bad conduct, neither did they inspire confidence. The vague odor of innocent brimstone around them was nevertheless dissipated at Saint-Méjean when Mother and Aunt Geneviève made the acquaintance of Madame Lhoumeau. Her excellent manners and her consummate skill at knitting (notably her mastery of the double cross-stitch) had definitely conquered them. Edmée Lhoumeau belonged to an old family connected with the legal profession in the Saintonge area. She had been educated at the Convent of the Dames of Saint-Maur. She was a stickler for good principles, so great a stickler that once and for all she had

chosen to close her eyes to the strains (which were, moreover, trifling) that her children could put on her principles.
As for the *children*, who were already no longer children
when our friendship was formed, they were admirably hypocritical, giving their parents as well as ours the impression
of having the most engaging manners, being perfectly polite to the point of attentiveness. I remember with an
impulse to laugh even now that Vincent went so far as to
kiss the ladies' hands, which greatly impressed Mother and
Aunt Geneviève. They did not know that hardly had he
turned on his heels after a supremely elegant hand-kissing
than he slipped into another role completely, that of a
rascal of good family, not disdaining extremely coarse language in declaring: "Women, my dear boy—if you want to
screw them, begin by kissing their hand," a formulation
whose scandalous insolence, quasi-sacrilegious, filled me
with both admiration and indignation.

I renewed acquaintance with Vincent and Julie at
Mother's burial after a long absence on Julie's part. Vincent
never failed to stop by when he came back to the area.
Monsieur Lhoumeau had retired from his position at the
bank. Long before that, he and his wife had bought an old
house on the banks of the Guirlonne, a dwelling suitable
for growing rosebushes and weeping willows, but also suitable for sustaining the rheumatism which Monsieur
Lhoumeau complained of when I would run into him at the
post office.

Vincent continued to cross my life as one fords a river,
from stone to stone, going from one strange kind of work to
an even more dubious occupation, but always casual and

with an elegance that was a bit too elegant, looking flashy and gayer than ever. He opened a *designer's* shop for pets, selling collars, wicker dog beds, blankets and toys for beloved poodles, loyal boxers, and expensive Persian cats. Then, after that failed, he worked in public relations on the staff of Edmond Saunier, a native of our town and the school dunce, later to become the pop star whose stage name was Cliff Stormer. Vincent then disappeared somewhere in Asia, and I next saw him again two years later one summer, suntanned and dressed in colonial garb of lightweight poplin. He had become rich as a kind of French Don Juan working as a promoter in a Sun Club on the islands of Lakdhar. He had been driven out of there only by a fire at the camp which had been caught unawares by a rebel ethnic group. The Lakdharian army had not brought things under control until after the massacre of a dozen European tourists whose throats had been cut by the rebels most ungallantly. The last news I have of him, Vincent spends the winters working in a discotheque in the Rue Saint Anne and the summers in the disco's place in Saint-Tropez.

Now and then I've had some rather vague news of Julie through him. Life's chance happenings are as incredible as those of a novel. In books the characters constantly meet one another accidentally. Nevertheless, I had not seen Julie again one single time until Mother's burial. I know that Julie came back frequently to see her parents in Marsac, but I never once ran into her in town. Vincent tells me that she has worked as a press agent for a well-known couturier, been an airline hostess on an ephemeral route of an ephemeral company called *Air San Marino*, married a rich

21

English alcoholic while insisting that the nuptial ceremony take place in the Russian church of Geneva, which was agreed to, only the God of the Orthodox Church knows how, although the groom was a Presbyterian and the bride a non-practicing Catholic. John, Julie's husband, succeeded in ruining himself by well-calculated speculation on the Stock Exchange, and then methodically devoted himself to killing himself with alcohol. He succeeded rather quickly. Julie looks a bit burned out by the whiskey shared during the years she spent with John and is now managing a bridge club in Paris. Vincent, with an indifferent insolence, implies that Julie doesn't only organize meetings between men and women bridge players, but also furthers other relationships. Over the years, Vincent has let the charming affected cynicism of his youth with which he loved to provoke me become a little coarse and heavy. One day when he came to Breuil and found me grappling with the bookkeeping for the operating costs, he shrugged his shoulders. "All the trouble you take just so your brother can play at being an important man." I protested. Olivier wasn't *playing* at being important, he really was one of the stars of the university. "Listen," said Vincent, "just between the two of us, your brother is a pretentious bastard. I leafed through his *Scriptology and Textology* at the bookstore. A lot of hot air! And the fact that he used to sleep with my sister doesn't change anything!"

I think Vincent thought that I had known that for a long time, but I hadn't. That's how I learned some years later that Julie who had made my heart quicken had . . .

It's an old story now, but I was a bit shaken when I heard it.

After Mother's death, a telegram announcing the arrival of Vincent and Julie came. Things didn't turn out as I had anticipated. Everybody had changed with the exception, no doubt, of myself, who had changed neither place nor being. Olivier has always had an air of assurance and of being more serious than his age merited. With time, these traits became more pronounced. As Vincent says, he has become his own statue. When he turns around, it isn't all of a piece, but all of a stone. He is the perfect image of the scholarly professor, the celebrated textologist, and no one could even imagine now, not even he himself, that once upon a time he and Julie . . .

My heart started beating as I saw Julie getting off the train. But it wasn't the Julie of the old photographs, the one that I had preserved intact in my mind, her blond ponytail pulled back with an elastic band, with scratches on her knees and all the boys hot on her heels, lit up at the sight like glow-worms on a warm August night. Julie has gotten fat, but the word *fat*, sad as it is, is not exactly right. She has become bloated. In the evening when he was alone with me, Vincent gave me a brief explanation: "Her job requires her to drink more than she should, and alcohol makes her swell up." She was wearing a knitted mohair coat of all the colors of a boreal autumn and a suit of lavender wool trimmed with navy blue silk with a neck opening where inexpensive necklaces, no doubt sophisticated, tinkled against a cream-colored silk blouse. But it was her

23

makeup that really struck me. It did not accentuate the fleshy features of this face that I once so greatly admired, but covered it with a violent, shiny, cruel mask. When she kissed me, she said: "I got some rouge on your cheek. Let me wipe it off." I tried to smile as I looked at her, but I wanted to be alone and cry. During the burial which, according to the customs of our province, was all in the lovely black of mourning, complete with black crepe veils, black suits, black dresses, and the funereal odor of mothballs floating over the cortège, Julie was the character in technicolor who had strayed into an old black and white film.

We stayed together only a few moments. She sat smoking in the little living room where old Marie had consented due to the circumstances to take off the white cotton dust covers. We exchanged a few meaningless phrases that quite clearly said nothing about the realities of our lives. Then Julie crushed out her cigarette in the bowl at the feet of a Dresden china shepherdess, a bowl decorated with blue waves of porcelain which had doubtlessly never before suffered such an affront. As she placed her hand on mine, she whispered in a rasping voice that with tenderness I would have called veiled and sad, "It's better this way, my dear Etienne. You see I was not the woman for you."

It may well be that Julie was not "the woman for me," the woman Mother and my aunts, I very well knew, talked about such a long time when they thought I wasn't listening. I was "presented" to her at least a dozen times, "the woman for me," with that fake normality of marrying families that, as if by enchantment, scatter throughout the house after a good Sunday dinner so that *these youngsters* can be alone. I think I used a half dozen of those famous tête-à-têtes with the eligible hopefuls with the heiress to the Dargeau property, with the eldest daughter of the Cornier domains, with the last little one of the Camaudon clan, or with the gentle and lovely lame youngest child of the Pirard des Sablon family, to leaf through my albums as amateur herbalist or, if they had a taste for literature, to have them visit my library. Things never went beyond that. Mother and my aunts finally were discouraged and sadly concluded that I would end up as a bachelor. For my own part, I figured I would end up as I had started out: I was born a bachelor and would remain a bachelor.

It was that bachelor twenty years old in the photographs who hopelessly gazes at Julie with her ponytail pulled back with an elastic band and her pale eyes that I always knew were green even though the snapshots are in black and white.

It was later on at the beginning of one summer that the person we had called "the American" all season long appeared in the family albums. Every time that the photo in which he first appears with us shows up as we turn the pages, Mother lets out the short dissonant cry that means for her a happy approval. From a distance, the American continues to enchant us as he enchanted all of us. He appeared on the beach one morning wearing a robe of black terrycloth and a bright blue bathing suit. He spread an orange-colored towel on the sand and when, after taking a sun bath, he ran toward the water and plunged in, he was no longer simply the newcomer, the stranger who drew everyone's attention, but the fine crawl swimmer and, if not exactly the athlete, at least the sportsman. He swims out quite far for a very long time and, back on dry ground, we watch him do cartwheels with the virtuosity of an acrobat and sit in the lotus position like a true yogi. Then he comes back and stretches out on the orange towel and closes his pale eyes, offering himself voluptuously to the sun. The beach now knows it must contend with this new swimmer.

I suspect Vincent and Julie, three days later, of having deliberately sent their balloon sailing toward the orange towel so that they could engage in conversation with the owner. Vincent had seen that he was reading a book in English. Consequently, he began speaking to him in English, and the stranger answered him in English. Vincent was proud of being able to carry on a conversation in that language, even if his English was much more chaotic than that of his interlocutor. Vincent told us that the stranger's name was Steven Sting, that he was an American, and that during the summer he lived at La Palud. Two days later, he presented Steven Sting to the mothers, who were delighted with his fine manners, by the French he spoke almost without accent, and by his handsome Anglo-Saxon looks, his short blond hair that curled a bit after swimming, his eyes of a pale Atlantic blue, and by his way of bending over so courteously before the women in a manner, alas, no longer practiced in France.

On that beach that was so French, so proper, slightly boring, the *American* created the happy quiver of something different. He was charming, our mothers said, and "so well brought up." We found him *formidable,* in the water and on dry land with his airs of an adolescent gentleman. But it was Mother, I believe, who most fully gave in to his charm.

Several days later, the American had become a member of our group. He had begun to give us lessons in swimming the crawl. He organized volleyball games on the beach and had Mother taste a drink made of lemon juice and honey. I had my first conversation with him. He was reading one of those solidly bound books so well edited in Anglo-Saxon countries. At that time they were the only kind of book. Pocket books still did not exist; they came with the war. I remember that the American was reading Samuel Butler's *Erewhon*, a book and an author I knew nothing about. As he was talking to me, I mechanically leafed through the book and saw that he had written his name on the cover page. It was not the one Vincent had told us, and that we had understood afterward, every time he pronounced it. Steven Sting's name was Stefan Stein. I was surprised to hear him say it with a smile, as if to excuse himself:

"I am not an American. I am German. I left Germany with my parents in 1934. I am Jewish."

· 3 ·

If I had not met Stefan, I no doubt would have had a tendency to whine and whimper over life. Moreover, and more often than I would like, I start, if not to complain (to whom could I complain?), at least to feel sorry for myself when no one can see me. But the very thought of Stefan keeps me from bemoaning my fate. The only real complaint I make about life is that my best friend is someone whom I never see, or at least so rarely and for such brief periods. I am quite certain, however, that Stefan is my best friend. He is sufficiently sensitive so that I cannot ask myself the question: am I his best friend or only one of his best friends? When we get together again after long intervals, he is so thoughtful and so affectionate a questioner that I feel exactly as I did when we first met, when, for the first time in my life I think, I had the feeling that I was *important* to someone. My brother put up with me. Mother nagged me. Father said nothing. I was usually the member of the family who was always there, whom you took for granted. No one paid any attention to me unless there was a need for me. Stefan taught me the luxury of existing in the eyes of someone else through and for myself.

Looking at me as he often does, with the objective eye of a doctor, Olivier said to me one day: "Etienne knows how to keep his friends: he chooses the ones who are absent." The malice is penetrating. It is easier to like each other from one end of the earth to the other when, as people say, you're not "on top of each other."

It's true that in the forty years since our meeting we have spent few days together. The war kept us apart until 1946 when Stefan came back to Europe for several weeks. He had just finished his law and philosophy studies. In Buenos Aires, he had found help from Professor Gutiérrez who had gone to great lengths to get a scholarship for him because of his father, and to find part-time work for him. Gutiérrez was about to get Stefan's naturalization for him.

Six years later, Stefan published his first book, *Law and History,* which was quickly translated into English and then into French, and, it seems, it created quite a stir in legal circles. I am not a philosopher, historian or jurist, so I must confess that a large part of Stefan's book is difficult for me to comprehend. I am, however, sensitive to the *tone* of many passages where I can discern the voice of my friend. The blending of cold tranquillity and of calm fury that he sometimes shows when confronting events of contemporary history, as if he were removing himself deliberately from them, constituted a carefully formed abstract of his ego, and once he had established his distance, allowed him to express an *objective* anger. Stefan came to Paris for the publication of his book in French, and he made a special trip to Breuil to see me.

Shortly after the publication of *The State of the Law and the Law of the State*, he married Nora Radcliff whom he brought to meet us when the literary award, Prix Minerva, was awarded to him in Frankfurt-am-Main. I saw Stefan again in 1967 when he was named *Doctor honoris causa* at the University of Oxford. Nora died a year later, leaving Stefan with a small daughter, Sara. I had no news from him for a long time after that. He obviously got back to work, as shortly before the last military coup in Argentina, he published his *The Anatomy of Injustice*. In my opinion, the opinion of a layman, it is his finest book.

I blush when I think that at sixteen or seventeen I had the ambition to write one day myself. My family smiled at this *vocation* that I had tried to keep a secret, but Mother was concerned. The true vocation in the family was my brother's. Olivier had the quiet assurance of someone who knows what he wants. I have the impression that for all eternity he had been destined for advanced studies, that he would go on to graduate work at the Ecole Normale and then teach there. Neither Mother, who was the regent of our clan, nor my father, who had no voice in things not connected with the properties, seemed to doubt for an instant that when Olivier prepared himself for a fine academic career, it would be my place to help my father and (as Mother said) to "get my hands into the batter." Olivier's hands were too delicate to even think of dirtying them, and his studies (later on to be called his *work*) too important for him to be bothered with agricultural chores. Consequently my life took the direction that everyone except myself had decided. I stayed on in Breuil after my *bachot*. Olivier went first to Poitiers and then to Paris to prepare his entrance exams for the Ecole Normale. He passed with high marks on his second try.

Mother had had a difficult time taking my *future* as a writer seriously. In her eyes, I didn't have the right to turn away from my responsibilities for *childish things*. Despite her lack of curiosity in matters of art and letters, she tried to inform herself, in case my *vocation* should persist, about writers for whom literature, even in cases of great success, had only been like Ingres' violin, a hobby that did not replace a serious career. Without giving any warning, she would introduce into the conversation an allusion to Chateaubriand who had written his books after long days of work as Ambassador of France. Or else, in a wholly unexpected burst of biographical erudition, she would make a point about Paul Valéry who had been an employee of a businessman almost all of his life before being named to the French Academy. I didn't say a word when faced with these lessons on the future and on proper conduct disguised as unexpected information and destined to remind me that I should never make light of the responsibilities that awaited me. I only protested quietly when Mother went a little too far and affirmed with the excess of the partially informed, based on badly misunderstood remarks, that Balzac had written his *The Human Comedy* during evenings when he had no work to do as director of a publishing company. I had to point out to Mother that Balzac's career as a printer

32

had only been a very short interlude, but I could not change her mind. She persisted in drawing a conclusion that concerned me from a fact with which I did not argue: Balzac had *also* been in business. "If he was a printer, that proves that even a writer can handle serious matters."

I bent my head and did not reply, but inside myself another me ironically shrugged his shoulders. The docile son accepted deferentially without appeal the verdict that strongly contrasted "things that are serious" to those that are not. But the other me, the rebel, sheltered by a hypocritical expression of acquiescence, did not in any way change his opinion to devote himself to all those things that Mother considered "not serious," which is to say what for me were my *sole necessities*.

And first of all, so as to escape the weight of the clan, I would not do my family the unmerited honor of associating their name with my future glory. I compiled lists of ten pen names and tried them out loud. I consulted atlases and etymological dictionaries, I put together romantic or rare first names like Tristan or Sandor or Marien with simple country names from around here like Marchois, Plantain or Chalemel. I went over them out loud and thought about taking a new name for myself, to rebaptize myself Ghislain or Urbain. I decided it would suffice to mask my surname while keeping the Etienne. I sounded the combinations of syllables for a long time until the day I finally made a definite decision and chose the name Georges d'Armillier, after a week of playing around with the root *ar*, which vaguely suggests an idea of joining, of organization or of arrangement, with a kind of sonority suspended between

33

arms, arm, armor, and a work of art, combined with the Sanskrit *imrab*, which means the arm of the body, or the Latin *arma*, the weapon arms, and *artes*, the arts, all of which would unite in defining my lofty destiny. It would be the destiny of an artist, a creator, of a combatant of the spirit; one of those hands at the pen that would be well worth the hand on the plow, and would surpass the coarse armed hand of the warrior. I repeated the phrases in which I pointed out the newcomer to the histories of literature: *"The work of Georges d'Armillier marks a turning point in the evolution of the French novel."* Or the following: *"With his very first works, Georges d'Armillier took his place effortlessly as one of the masters of the new French prose."* Thus acclaimed, but by myself alone, and even before having published anything, crowned secretly before having competed, I played at taking a glory upon myself without having done anything that would indicate whether I would merit any such praise or not.

As a matter of fact, I have never merited such praise, and I must say that I have never really tried to acquire it. But it was Stefan who became what I would have aspired to become. When I dreamed of writing, it was merely a *childish daydream,* and what spurred me on was the simple need to affirm: I am here, listen to me. For Stefan, what he had to say went much, much farther. I comprehended him one day when, after a year of conversations and confidences, he finally told me one summer afternoon about the day during his fourteenth year that had *marked* his destiny forever.

I had taken Stefan to go fishing that day. The water of

our Guirlonne, neither lively nor dormant, flows lazily, and if our little river was lazy, our fishing was no less so. Simple fishing with a pole has nothing adventurous about it. I rowed our little flat-bottomed boat over to the mooring pole on the other bank. Then we dropped minced bait into the deepest hole and fixed our rods in the earth after we had baited the hooks. There's nothing more to do then except to wait until there's a bite. We were comfortably installed on the riverbank in a couple of natural seats that had been hollowed out and shaped by generations of fishermen before us.

"We could almost go to sleep if we had a little bell," said Stefan.

"You're not far off saying that. Around here we do fishing with a cattle bell. The fisher can snooze away quietly. If a fish bites, the bell wakes him up, unless it's a water plant or a piece of debris of some kind that makes it ring."

On the banks of the sluggish Guirlonne, Stefan told me about the afternoon when he was fourteen, one day beside a much swifter and colder stream, in Germany at Scherchensee. He had not forgotten a single moment or a single detail of that July day. Neither have I forgotten anything of his story. After that, he alluded to it only very rarely and very indirectly, as though once he had confided to me the images of a day when his life, like a door that closes, had pivoted for all time on its hinges, he had given me proof of his confidence and (perhaps) the beginnings of a deliverance, or at least of sharing. But who was I, an insignificant Frenchman from a moderately hilly countryside, an insignificant bumpkin from a region of sleepy streams, a poor countryman of limited horizons, to be faced with that outburst of violence that would never fully reach me personally, but that I would only experience indirectly as a kind of repercussion?

· 4 ·

That morning, said Stefan, at the age of fourteen, I was all sorts of truly interesting people: a gold prospector in the snows of Alaska cracking his whip over the heads of six ferocious and faithful huskies, or a treasure hunter in the South Seas, looking for gold doubloons hidden in 1623 on one of the islands of the Requin Archipelago by One-Eyed Jack and his crew, a week before they were captured by the Royal British Navy and hanged high and dry from the main yard of the HMS *Generous*.

That morning, going between my parents' and Kurt's parents' chalets, my bicycle became by turns a huge motor-cycle whose motor zoomed loudly (I imitated the sound with my mouth), a polo pony (I was the elegant quick horseman, giving an adroit kick to the polo balls—that is, the pine cones scattered on the roadway—as I went by), and finally, going downhill, I became the head of a bobsled team winning the last competitions of winter, the captain whose quiet authority transformed the four men (two hundred pounds each, nothing but muscle, not an ounce of fat) into one single body dizzily perched on the sled's edge as we headed straight down the slope.

My fishing rod and equipment were solidly fastened to my bike along the crossbar and in the saddlebags and the side baskets.

Among the fir trees and on down in the valley, there was a light mist from the heat that precedes the first very hot days between springtime and summer. It is the moment when the earth is still saturated from the long rains of the end of winter, but when the sun is already strong enough to be quite hot. How good it is to breathe the cool air mixed with delicate spray of water, to feel the humid caress of the mist on one's face and arms. It's a time when the river's water is covered with tufts of steam in the silence of the still raw morning.

Kurt was outside waiting for me in front of his parents' chalet so that I wouldn't have to knock at the door and wake up the sleepers.

Every time we met, we stood face to face and put the palms of our hands together, then slapped them cross-wise. Then we both spoke the secret passwords: *"Abra! Tabra! Babra! We are of the same blood, you and I!"*

We had read *The Jungle Book* six months earlier. As for the three cabalistic words, that was our secret language. We had sworn over the flame of a fir brand never to reveal them to anyone under pain of ostracism and banishment, punishments learned from the lessons in ancient history from our professor Herr Fritz Müller.

We had agreed to eat breakfast that morning at Kurt's house, because the Reichbach chalet was bigger than ours and the kitchen was somewhat more isolated, so that way we would not disturb our parents who, during vacation time, slept later than usual. We also enjoyed fixing our own breakfast. The habit of mothers and maids of doing everything for boys is beneficial for laziness, but can be distasteful for dignity.

We had fixed everything that we didn't normally have when we were with our parents, that is, very strong coffee, without any chicory but with more sugar than was usually permitted, and one single dish served not in the regular bowls but in what we could find that was bigger—small dishes for salad that were larger than the largest bowls. We tossed in quite a mixture: rolled oats, crackers, raisins, leftover chocolate rice pudding that we found in the icebox, milk, honey, whipped cream, powdered sugar, and two apples cut into thin slices. It was enormous, gigantic, succulent, overflowing, nourishing, excessive, disgusting— in short, delicious. We gulped down that mess without saying a word, like two cats licking leftovers, and as we drank our boiling-hot bowls of coffee, we felt fine. When the two real cats of the house came in from their nightly excursions, there was nothing left for them in the salad bowls, and Kurt gave them some milk.

Kurt's picnic lunch was all prepared in a big clean cloth slipped into a canvas container. He put it in his knapsack. "Shall we go? It's going to get good and hot."

The mist began to lift even among the fir trees, and when we got to a clearing between them, we could see the river down below, a placid mirror from which the last wisps of vapor ascended here and there. We made our descent free-

39

wheeling and unprotected, down among the pastures and the still pale fields of oats. Larks were singing their hearts out without missing a breath. I remember that up in the dark blue sky there was a single white cloud, a long scarf of indolent soapsuds that we watched float slowly on very high up.

"Let's race, but no pedaling! The first one down wins, but no cheating. All right?" "All right," said Kurt.

The fine clickety-clack of a well-oiled hub and the zestful wind in one's ears is an intoxicating experience, and neither one of us won, because we both weighed the same and were of the same blood, Kurt and I. We began to pedal again with strong legs and the great chivalrous good humor of champion cyclists, the Titans of Bicycle Racing that we had read about in the sports pages, or imitating the gods of Olympus in the Latin versions given to us by Herr Fritz Müller.

We got off our bikes when we reached the meadow. The grass was strewn with red and white clover, and riddled with grasshoppers that crackled under our feet. There was a screen of willows, alders, and beeches along the stream. We pushed our bikes willy-nilly in the field as far as the beaten path that goes along the river. The river is deep there, and the closer to the middle, the darker the water, almost a clear black, a kind of blackness to the water because there is a bottom, but that one feels is clear, pure and cold, because it is formed by rivulets and streams that come down from the mountains. If you look at it where the riverbanks are not steep, on a bottom of sand and gravel that gently descends, the water is transparent, and you can see the schools of minnows looking like racers at the starting line as they swim counter-current, and you think you glimpse a big fish, a carnivorous creature of the water, crossing between light and shadow. The opaque water reflects the lazy cloud that glides along the water with the current's flow, looking like a white linen scarf or a cream-colored zeppelin, or a cigar of foam.

We got back on our bikes and took the riverside path upstream. It was already very hot, and the river swallows were flying high overhead. I heard an invisible warbler in the beech trees. "Let's stop and listen." The bird begins its song softly, a discreet warbling as if it were searching for its voice, then trills an aria like a flute, the notes climbing the scale, the bird itself astonished by what comes out of its throat, and it stops on a *forte*, a tenuous note as high as the voice can go. I said, "It's a black-headed warbler," with the applied modesty of the truly wise naturalist. At that time I was very proud of the fact that I could identify birds, plants, flowers, and trees. At school, I was number one in natural sciences.

I decided that we would go to the place where the smaller stream flows into the river, where there is a wooden footbridge. "It's a spot that the *fish* like, because the water is colder there than anywhere else." I was the chief that morning, the one who was the most knowledgeable, who knew what we had to do. Kurt understood that, and he was in agreement.

Our footsteps frightened a water rat that was foraging along the bank. He hurried off in the water fluttering his paws, and we could see nothing more than his snout and his two shiny close-set eyes, and from the point of his nose backward, the wake of a V.

We set our bikes against some willows on the stream's bank where the water is no longer quite transparent. The grass was strewn with pussy willows. We spread out a large square of tent canvas in the shade and began to undo our equipment after having arranged our picnic provisions in the cool shade of the bushes and put our canteens to chill in the cold of the running water. At the edge of the bank there was some watercress, and we were sorry we hadn't brought some salad oil with us. With some lemon juice and salt, watercress is very good.

I lined up my equipment on the canvas as much for the purpose of taking inventory of my treasures and to be able to admire the objects one by one as to be orderly and methodical: the handful of corks, the two pieces of the bamboo rod that screw together, the reel with the turning drum, the coarse hair and gut string, the sinkers of various calibres, the hook kit, the bait-spoons, the lures, the box of black-headed worms, and the landing net, all of which made Kurt's eyes pop.

"Your father did a great job!"

"My reward for excellence last year was the bike. This year, my father says he's going to make a real fisherman out of me. He's always afraid I'll end up sitting on my butt doing nothing but reading. He wants me to be an athlete too, *mens sana in corpore sano,* he says."

The sun had risen higher in the sky and was hotter and hotter through the leaves. There was a light breeze, however, and the sun's rays played at movements on the grass, on our faces, on the metal of objects that mirrored little silver beams.

I explained to Kurt: "You'll see. It's a question of thought and skill. You choose the equipment according to the spot, the hour and the depth of the water. . . . And I'll show you how to get the knack of casting. . . . It isn't hard. . . ."

Obviously I was using a rather solemn tone, the slow precision of the pedagogue, with the patience to explain things clearly.

I prepared the rod and the line and explained it to Kurt step by step. Why one chooses this thickness of line and sinkers of this weight—in relationship to the current near the riverbank—why, rather than a hook or a grasshopper you use a worm that you have to thread with care and change it often because it gets off the hook. We're going to try a bait-spoon of white metal first, one that will be fully visible and brilliant in the darker water. We're going to regulate the reel so that the lure will spin out at the right pace, and there's no risk of snapping the line.

I gave a demonstration for Kurt, casting the line eight or ten meters, then reeled in the line slowly as I moved the rod in little zig-zags. "That way your lure has the pace of a real fish that isn't moving mechanically, but hesitates, changes its mind, rests a moment and then goes on . . ."

I said: "Now you try" as I passed the rod to Kurt. Naturally Kurt got his line caught in a tree behind us and then missed his second cast and landed the sinkers and bait-spoon on the riverbank where they got stuck in the moss. But without getting excited I had Kurt go through the movements again, with patience. He's less dextrous than I, but he applies himself, and I'll make a real rod and reel fisher out of him.

I put the extra equipment we might need into the satchel, pieces of fishing line, sinkers, bait-spoon, while Kurt took charge of the landing net and the basket for our catch. We arranged everything else in the saddlebags of the bicycles and fastened the wheels with security chains. "At any rate, if we go on down-river, we can see the bikes we're leaving here. No risk at all."

We decided we would fish in turn as we went along the river, then we would come back to our "camp" to swim and eat our lunch. The one who wasn't casting had to carry the net, the extra equipment, the bucket full of little fish, if we were to decide to fish with live bait, and the box of worms, if that was what worked best.

As we went upstream, we had the sun on one side, the kind of sun that climbs slowly, but whose rays don't come straight down. They ricochet and rebound on the surface of the water instead of down into it. The cool of the morning had completely evaporated, but the air was still not burning hot as we had expected it would be at noon. We both looked at the gentle curve of the river, and of the path and bank that we were going to follow. We felt like a ship's crew ready for the cast-off at the beginning of a great adventure on a beautifully generous morning that opened out before us. We had carefully articulated the sacred words together: *"Abra! Tabra! Babra! We are of the same blood, you and I!"* "Shall we go?"

I remember that there was a large enclosed meadow there

with a single bull in it that came over to look at us from the other side of the wall snorting through his nose, looking mean. There were some hazel trees there, but the nuts were not yet ripe. On the other side of the river there was a field of wheat that had already turned yellow and up above it a lark that succeeded in staying in place by beating her wings so rapidly that she seemed to be in articulate balance with her song, but she began zig-zagging crazily and let herself fall like a stone into the wheat because a buzzard was lurking above her. I explained to Kurt that she surely had her nest in the field, but she went elsewhere, far away from it, using cunning to lead the buzzard away from her little ones.

It was beginning to get very hot. There was a continuous faint buzzing in the air from bees, midges, hornets, mosquitoes, and those big blue dragonflies with their big round eyes and transparent silken wings that fly in fits and starts, suddenly changing directions and tacking. And the quiet and delicate whirring of the reel when we pulled in the fishing line.

I remember it was Kurt who caught the first fish. We had both cast several times, but either the creature let go too quickly or it was not a real bite, and twice we pulled in grass attached to the hook. But that time it really was a fish, and we were very excited, but a true fisherman is calm and the master of himself. I talked to Kurt quietly, as if raising my voice would scare the fish away. "Easy now, let out some slack, then pull in again. . . . Tire it out. . . ." He had the net in his hand, and when Kurt brought his maneuvering to

45

an end with both anguish and joy, I took hold of the creature that was still struggling, but it was not a trout but only a large dace.

We went slowly back up the river. There were some cows that were watching us from the other side, then a farmer on his mechanical mower who was talking to his horse. The odor of freshly cut hay could be smelled across the river. And there was a kingfisher flung like a stone of turquoise and fire that went into the water like an arrow and came back out with the shining silver of a small fish in its beak. There was another fisherman, a bearded gentleman in a boat who was wearing a Tyrolean hat, and who said hello to us as his boat floated slowly downstream with the current. The birds were silent now, and the murmur of insects filled the morning which now drew toward its midday heat.

An invisible fish approached the lure, teased it and tested it. I reeled too late, or badly, and ended up with nothing. The spoon and the hook got stuck in a stump under the water, and after several tries at unfastening it, I had to cut the line and bring it in without either hook or spoon. I decided to try fishing with live bait. I grabbed an unfortunate tiny minnow in the bucket and carefully attached it by the nose, feeling a bit disgusted but manfully overcoming my sentimental reaction. A fisher is a man, and he should not let himself think like a weakling. (But I was thinking to myself: all the same, what if some giant was picking me up in his fingers and putting a pointed hook through my nose. What would I feel?)

Far off we heard the sound of the twelve strokes of noon on the clock of Fertigheiligen, and it was five minutes later (it was Kurt's turn to cast) that the big one bit hard enough to shake the line. We each did our bit without getting unnerved. I explained to Kurt what he had to do, and Kurt did it. "Let out a little line. . . . Strike hard. . . . You've got him. . . . Let out more line. . . . Turn the reel three or four times. . . . You can see him. . . . It's a . . . It's pulling . . . Give it some slack, then tighten . . . Here's the net . . . Try to get it in sideways . . . Watch the grass on the left . . . I'm coming . . . I've got it. . . ."

Twisting and turning like a devil caught in the mesh of the landing net, then arching its back and flopping on the grass, there was the most beautiful fish in the world, the most beautiful fish that any fisher ever fished. It was only twenty-five or thirty centimeters long, but it was a trout, our trout, a bluish gray trout with pale rose and red speckles. I was trembling a bit with emotion as I tried to unhook the jaw without tearing the flesh. I gave the creature a sharp rap on the head, holding it from underneath, so that it would die quickly without suffering, but fishing is fishing. It was certainly the most beautiful fish in the world, and certainly the most beautiful trout of our whole lives. We looked down at the trout which was no longer moving. Only the gills seem to be still rising. No, it's over. *"Abra! Tabra! Babra!"* (clapping our crossed hands) *"We-are-of-the-same-blood-you-and-I."*

And like all things that have their time of full flower and then close up, fade and pass away, the trout already had lost the brightness of the first moment. Its colors were fading away, its bright shine was becoming blurred, and its scales were turning dull. Our trout began no longer to be wholly our Most Beautiful Fish in the World, but just a dead fish which already was beginning to smell of fish. We put it in the basket, surrounded it with wet leaves, and returned in modest triumph to our "camp."

We went swimming where the cavorting stream flows into the river. It was fun to swim from the cold water of the river into the even colder water of the tributary, and we made some bets on who could stay longest under water without breathing, and then threw to the bottom a pebble that we had to try to find. We raced each other from the "camp" to the other riverbank, and we discovered the opening of a tunnel-nest of a kingfisher hidden under the stump of an alder. We went back upstream as far as a copse of reeds, frightening a sedge-warbler that flew off with a cry of indignant protestation and a great rustling of wings and rushes.

Then we climbed onto the bank and stretched out on the grass in the sun to dry ourselves. When we were quite dry and warm, we put on our undershirts, got out our provisions and pulled the canteens from the water. We installed ourselves in the shade and undid the food. We were good and hungry, and we were happy, because there was plenty to eat, and very good things, and a variety, because each of us had been given different things, and so, by dividing between us, we had a sumptuous repast. There were hard-boiled eggs with salt, little tomatoes the shape of rugby balls, dry sausage cut into thin slices, and chicken sandwiches of white meat lightly seasoned with taragon mustard, with salad greens and rice pudding in an aluminum container, plus goat's milk cheese with cumin, and two big baskets of fruit, a bar of chocolate, and rye bread with sesame seeds. We had lemonade in one canteen and cool water in the other that was flavored by a powder to taste of anise and tea. We could have made a fire and grilled our fish with the thyme and sage that grew in the fields, but we preferred to go home to our parents with the trout, modestly, so as to hear them exclaim with surprise and admiration. Consequently we ate our provisions, carefully chewing every mouthful, with the pleasure that hunger gives the appreciation of two connoisseurs, as the less our hunger, the greater our appreciation of what we were eating. Afterward we felt like sleeping. We stretched out the canvas so that our feet would be in the sun and our bodies in the shade, and so we calculated how the sun would move, and then plunged into the warmth of midday on a lovely July day and into the tepid milk of sleep. Sometimes a fly would land on our foreheads, and a hand would unconsciously shoo it away. We slept without dreaming, deep in the womb of summer and the gentle rocking of the siesta. That day, the earth, that moment, were a cradle for me, an affirmation of being, and the happy respite accorded to those who have done what they had to do. Despite the wet leaves, the trout in the basket was already rigid. The earth circled the solar fire. A green grasshopper landed on my stomach and then jumped off into the grass.

I heard the motorcycle in my sleep. It was still far away, but it must have attacked some obstacles because the motor suddenly roared and backfired in the exhaust pipe. Then the machine came closer. It must have been going along the bank. The big black motorcycle stops in front of us, and

Laurel and Hardy are there. Hardy is holding the handle-bars, and he cuts off the ignition. He lowers the kickstands of the cycle while Laurel gets off the tandem-saddle. They slowly come toward us. They aren't Laurel and Hardy, because the real Laurel doesn't have the carnivorous jaw of the blond fellow, nor the eyes the color of an oyster with the blurred reflection, and the real Hardy is a fat guy like the other one, but he is rather craftily debonair while the fat one standing in front of us with his fringe of hair on his forehead almost down to the shoe-button eyes, and with his jowls the color of Nuremberg ham, this fat man excites fear rather than laughter. Laurel and Hardy are about eighteen years old. They are bigger than we are, and seem even more so because they are on their feet right in front of the two of us who have just been startled out of our sleep.

"What are you doing here?" asks Hardy.

"We're fishing."

"Who gave you the authorization to fish?" asks Laurel.

"I didn't know that. . ."

"When I speak to you, it isn't polite to answer while you're sitting down," says Hardy.

"On your feet!" says Laurel.

We got up. Once we were standing up, we didn't know exactly what to do or how to behave.

"So that's how you fish, eh?" says Hardy.

"Yes."

"Without any authorization?"

"We didn't know you had to have an authorization."

"Now you know," said Laurel.

"The next time we'll ask for an authorization!"

"Who will you ask for the authorization?" said Hardy, with a look of delight at having hit on something.

"I don't know."

Hardy turns toward Laurel and says: "You hear that, Rudi? He doesn't know!"

"He'll have to learn," said Laurel in a voice that sounded both distressed and threatening.

"The next time you want to go fishing," said Hardy, "You'll come ask for the authorization from me."

"But I don't know where you live!"

"No matter," said Hardy. "I won't give you the authorization anyway."

"Why not?"

"Because Jews aren't allowed to fish in a German river full of German fish," said Hardy.

When you look at him closely, Laurel does not resemble Laurel at all. The Laurel of the comic films has a good head of soft rubber. This one here is all hard bone, hollow and angled, blond, colorless, with a head like a weasel's or a polecat's. And he only looks like Laurel because from far off the fat one makes you think of him as compared to Hardy, but this one would be a Hardy of pure pork, with small eyes that are really deceitful, and even more deceitful when you see that there is one of them that's crossed. He squints, but the eye is so small that you don't see it right away.

Laurel has a painfully surprised look on his face. He cautiously interrogates Hardy:

"Did I get that right, Gustave? These two here were fishing German fish in a German river?"

"That's right," said Hardy.

51

"And you say they're Jews?"

"As Jewish as you can be," said Hardy. "This one's the son of that sheeny professor Friedrich Stein, and that one is as big a Yid as his friend."

Hardy turns to Stefan:

"You have to come ask for permission from your superior, from me, Gustave Schliemeier. Does that tell you something? My mother was the washwoman at your folks' place. She washed the Jew laundry for your tribe of sheenies. You remember Maria? That's my mother, working like a slave for the people of Israel. That's all over now."

Then he rapped out his words:

"You'll come to ask me for permission, and of course, I won't give it to you."

We stand there not saying a word.

"What'll you come to ask me for?" asks Laurel in a threatening voice.

Hardy takes a step forward and slowly slaps my face.

"What'll you come to ask me for?" Hardy repeats.

"It's not polite not to answer when somebody asks you something in a nice way," said Laurel.

"Well, you going to answer?" asks Hardy.

"You'd better answer," says Laurel. "When Gustave hits, he hits hard."

Laurel turns toward Hardy and imitates a well-educated man courteously asking a small favor.

"Will Gustave grant me permission to teach the Jew Stein some manners? I have a persuasive way about me that, in a way, is more delicate than Gustave's."

"He's all yours," says Hardy.

Laurel deliberately hits me twice.

"What will you come to ask me for?" Hardy says again.

I stammer a wholly useless phrase, as I well know: "You have no right!"

Hardy looks at Laurel with profound stupefaction.

"Did you hear what he said?"

"He's talking about rights, is that it?" says a painfully surprised Laurel in an incredulous voice.

"Would you have ever thought of such a thing, Rudi, a Jew who pollutes a German river full of German fish, and who has the gall to talk about *rights*?"

Hardy is indignant. His voice rises.

"But with what right do you talk about rights, you vermin? We catch you in the act, thumbing your nose at the law of the Reich, and you have the gall to pronounce the word *rights*! If you're going to talk like that, I'll show you how to conform to German law! Show me your identity papers."

We look at each other.

"You don't have any papers?" said Hardy. "You dare go fishing in a German river without papers? But I'm good-natured. Show me your pricks and that'll do."

We look at Laurel and Hardy, the two police on patrol.

"You get it? Your sheeny dicks, your Yid cocks, your circumcised glans. This time, we'll let it go with that for your identity papers."

There is a long silence.

"We're waiting," says Hardy. "We're waiting for a good-will gesture!"

Another long silence.

Laurel and Hardy come toward me.

"Let me alone!"

Hardy grabs me from behind and twists my arm. Laurel takes down my bathing suit and takes out my penis. I struggle, but he has a tight hold on me.

"A weeny guaranteed to be Jewish. Not much to brag about, but beyond doubt belonging to the Jews."

"You ought to be ashamed," says Kurt when Hardy lets go of me. Tears were running down my face mixing with the snot I have no handkerchief to wipe from my nose.

"Shut your trap and show us your prick," Laurel says to Kurt.

Kurt starts to run, but Laurel and Hardy took off after him. Laurel has gotten ahead of him and trips him.

Hardy twists Kurt's arms. Laurel pulls his bathing suit down and takes Kurt's penis in his hands.

"I'll wash my hands afterward," he says. "A Jew's prick is dirty, but now we have the proof."

They let Kurt go. They pay no more attention to us, but start to go through our things.

"A German trout and dace in a Jewish basket? Confiscated by decision of the service for the control of the activities of Jews." Hardy empties the contents into one of the saddlebags of his motorcycle. Laurel is busy carefully breaking the bamboo fishing rod over his knees. He throws the sinkers, the hooks, the lures, and the bait piece by piece into the river. He is just about to toss the reel into the water when he changes his mind and puts it into the other saddlebag of the motorcycle.

"I hope now you've got the picture? You won't come here

any more without authorization to fish for German fish in a German river that's off-limits to Jews," says Laurel.

"You'll come to ask my permission and I'll deny it," says Hardy.

They have climbed onto their motorcycle, Hardy starts it up, and the motor backfires. They raise their arms in the Nazi salute.

"Heil Hitler!"

They go on their way down the path, revving their motor.

Our tears flow. There we stand, ashamed, silent, in the middle of the havoc of our camp with the pieces of the broken fishing rod. The sun, still burning hot, is beginning to go down. The afternoon is heading toward the dusk of a beautiful summer's day. A beautiful day for trout fishing.

· 5 ·

Stefan's appearance on the La Conche beach at Saint-Méjean had an unexpected consequence. I discovered my father, or at least I heard his voice. He talked so little that ordinarily Olivier said jokingly that, contrary to appearances, our father was not mute. He was heard talking once in 1935 while Mother was away. It is true that to bring Mother's word-mill to a halt, you had to have unflinching determination and to make a decisive attack during a pause in a sentence. My father had given up a long time ago.

Stefan quickly became a member of our group. He played volleyball with us, he taught the secrets of a tree's vertical growth to Vincent and Julie, introduced Olivier to chess, and if Grandmother wanted to wind some wool into a ball, he offered his two arms to hold the skein and helped by slowly oscillating the yarn to flow toward the ball. We learned that Stefan's father was a professor of natural sciences, and that he worked at the Ornithological Observation Station at Moustiers, a few kilometers from Saint-Méjean. Monsieur and Madame Stein lived in the village of Moustiers in a fisherman's house that served as a residence for the researchers employed at the station. Mother was dying to meet Stefan's parents. She had no prejudices, except for those unconscious prejudices that she expressed wth perfect innocence. She disguised her curiosity in the less frivolous guise of charity: "We should invite the parents of our German friend. It would be a kind act toward these poor people who have lost everything. Besides, their son is very well brought up. He's Jewish, but he's utterly charming."

Professor Ernst Friedrich Stein must have been about sixty. He was tall and thin, bald, tanned by sun and wind, and dressed in the kind of knickers cyclists wore in 1900 stuffed into stockings of indeterminate color. His jackets were the type mountain huntsmen wore, the kind with pockets bristling with notebooks and pens, and he always had on walking shoes with laces, replete with gussets and tongues and triple non-skid soles, and was armed with binoculars that never left him. Madame Stein, with her gray eyes that looked both benevolent and somewhat frightened blinking behind thick glasses, always seemed to be a half-step behind her husband.

At the end of the first Sunday dinner to which the Steins were invited, my father and the Professor got into a conversation that lasted two hours. They had discovered that in April 1917 they were both near Heurtebise during the offensive of Nivelle. They had suffered from the same cold in winter, trudged through the same mud and known the same fears. My father had had the "good luck" to be wounded in the shoulder blade and evacuated who knows why to Lourdes where (he explained, scandalizing Mother) "the Virgin had too much to do with the stiffs to think about miracles for the living." Professor Stein was not as "lucky." He had to wait six months before catching an almost fatal typhoid that brought about his evacuation to the rear.

My father and the Professor had similar reminiscences and converging interests. They relived the war as they talked about it, and they compared agricultural problems and the study of nature in Germany and France. During the fall and winter following our meeting Stefan at La Conche, the Steins got into the habit of coming to spend every other weekend in Breuil. Mother definitely found them charming, without any more *buts*. Stefan, who had spent the preceding years in Paris, had stayed on in Moustiers with his parents. He had enrolled in the university at Poitiers and went there two days a week for his coursework.

Olivier was in Paris attending a preparatory class for the Lycée Henry IV, and that left Stefan and me as the only ones the same age in Breuil.

Doctor Professor Ernst Friedrich Stein had taught Stefan three things in his childhood. The first thing was there is nothing more important than knowledge except honesty. Teachers must be respected at school, books and notebooks must be carefully bound in paper wrappers, and when you are asked whether you washed your ears and brushed your teeth, you tell the truth, even if it causes you trouble.

Professor Stein then taught Stefan that birds preceded man on the earth by at least a hundred and fifty million years, and that they have a good chance of being still here when man no longer is. According to him, that alone justified his having devoted his life to the study of them, but also elucidated the third point in the Professor's enlightenment of his son: to wit, that Darwin had described the world appreciably better than the Bible, which nevertheless retains considerable poetic interest. Ernst Friedrich went on to say that to talk about creation, God, sin, and eternal life was to deal with concepts that have little sense, but that people who took those concepts seriously should never be contradicted, beginning with Emma, his wife, Stefan's mother. Emma still was a believer. She prayed. He who believes has need to believe, said the Professor, and there is at least one highly valid project of Marx and Engels (otherwise very controversial, especially when they get into the field of natural sciences) and that is the need to give to each according to his needs. The needs of the soul are no less imperative than those of the organism, although quite as difficult to define and to foresee.

Emma Stein had taught Stefan two things: that his father was a man to be admired and loved, and that he should never be contradicted when he expressed doubts about the existence of the Everlasting. All that was necessary was to pretend to agree with him so that he could keep his opinion and we could keep ours. The fact that the Professor was a deeply pious man even if had no religious beliefs should never be forgotten. Emma encompassed in that word *piety* all of the virtues that she admired: generosity, rigor, self-lessness, and even that distraction that makes the presence of a timid spouse so very useful, a spouse that is capable of having her eyes open who still holds her tongue.

As his research was primarily devoted to the study of

marine birds and those inhabiting swampy areas, Ernst Friedrich made frequent and distant trips. The laboratory of ornithological studies at his university had sent him frequently to Africa and South America. Hitler became chancellor of the Reich while the Professor was studying a deposit of mummified and petrified small Hornby petrels that had been discovered in holes in the ground in the Gran Chaco desert. When he "returned to civilization," Ernst Friedrich was stupefied to find that National Socialism had taken over power in Germany from then on. He had never thought that such a thing could happen. The Professor belonged to that category of men for whom what is absurd is improbable, and what is irrational cannot come to pass. One of his American colleagues, who was working with him on the studies they were carrying out on the Hornby petrel in the desert, recalls that that night Professor Stein was nevertheless relatively optimistic. He thought that the scientific community at least would be sheltered from political upheavals.

Nevertheless, there was daily information that an important position in research or an endowed chair had switched professors: birds were also mobilized for service to "German science," and the unscrupulously ambitious took over their winter plumage.

The Professor was deprived of his chair several weeks after his return. His favorite student, who had been first his assistant and then his critic and denouncer, took his place. He had just joined the National Socialist Party and began his course with a "scientific" denunciation of Jewish ornithology. That was what caused Ernst Friedrich to start

61

thinking about emigrating. He received permission to leave on condition, of course, that he leave all his belongings behind. He would have done so without distress had it not been for giving up his library. In his exile in France during his long periods of insomnia, Professor Stein saw again certain of the books he had lost forever, the thirty volumes on birds of America by Audubon, the irreplaceable monograph of von Heinzel on the Tasmanian red-beaked cormorant, and an original edition of a collection of engravings of birds by Hokusai that had been presented to him in Tokyo when he had been invited to Japan in 1927 to give the Mishimoto lectures at the College of Sciences.

Shortly before their departure from Germany, Emma Stein astonished her family by a decision she made in secret from her husband. She followed the advice of her cousin Bacharach who was a businessman. She sold her jewels and everything of value in their apartment and bought a rare and valuable stamp from Sierra Leone, then took the risk of sending it in a letter to a French colleague of Ernst Friedrich, one Professor Lemire. Emma won her wager: the stamp went through without incident. The Stein family was able to subsist for several months after its arrival in Paris thanks to the sale of the stamp.

France, which was incapable of providing a professorial chair for Albert Einstein, obviously could not find one for a German ornithologist who specialized primarily in studies of the innate and acquired behavior of different species of petrels, frigates, and fulmars of the oceans of the world. Lemire and his colleagues tried hard to get work for Stein, usually unworthy of him but which nevertheless brought him a certain remuneration (inadequate, of course). "The eminent professor" thus took "vacations"; he would go to spend time in the ornithological stations in the Pyrenees Mountains or in the south in the Camargue, working at keeping count of migrating species and carrying out himself the numerous tasks that for years he had turned over to students. The Steins also received a modest monthly income from an American Jewish organization for assistance to the refugees from the Third Reich. They lived in two small rooms in a pension belonging to the Gevaudeau family in the Rue Gay-Lussac in Paris, eating their noonday meal in a restaurant in Montparnasse organized by a *Comité antifasciste pour les intellectuels allemands émigrés.* In the evening, Emma prepared their café-au-lait with a bit of cold cuts and bread over a gas-burner.

At the age of twelve, in the lull between childhood and adolescence, between Weimar and the Third Reich, Stefan and his best friend Kurt had taken their password from the formula of the *Jungle Book:* "*We are of the same blood, you and I.*" They did not give it the same meaning that the Nazis would have. Blood and race did not exist for them yet. In Paris, quickly on his own, there was another phrase of Kipling that would characterize Stefan, one whispered by the Cat of the *Just So Stories:* "*I am the cat who walks by himself, and all places are alike to me.*"

Despite having landed on the streets of Paris almost without resources and having grown too fast, badly nourished and still wearing short pants and clothes of foreign make, with a meager French studied in school that he could barely speak, Stefan had two clear objectives from his first days in France: long French pants and the complete mastery of the French language. Joseph, the son of Madame Gevaudeau who had the hotel where the Steins were living, was two years older than Stefan and already helped his mother. He did the accounting, took care of the reception desk, and answered the phone. Joseph felt sorry for the little German. Emma discovered to her horror and admiration that her son got up at five-thirty in the morning to go to the corner shop to pick up a bag filled with some hundred copies of the daily paper and a list of the subscribers to be delivered from door to door and floor to floor between six- and seven-thirty A.M. He earned three francs for that. He did not know the laws of supply and demand in the work-place or that he had taken the place of a little French boy who was paid twice as much, but whose demand for more money had lost him his job. Joseph had advised Stefan to go buy some secondhand clothes in the Flea Market or at the Salvation Army, but Stefan wanted to be a Frenchman dressed in new things. Joseph then advised him to wait for the January sales. Stefan's knees were cold, and he felt ridiculous, but finally he came back one day to the little Gevaudeau place in his first gray suit, purchased on sale at a shop named Alba with money he had earned himself. One thought spoiled his pleasure: wouldn't he grow too fast and look ridiculous again in a suit that was too short for him? He would have liked to have had Alice's magic mushroom from Wonderland, the one you only had to take a well calculated nibble of in order to grow taller or smaller at will. He would have stayed at the size of his suit.

At the restaurant of the antifascist intellectuals, Stefan

had read an announcement saying that there were free classes in French being given every morning in rooms of the local of the CGTU in the Rue Lafayette. He went there the next day. An office had been transformed into an improvised classroom, with tables that served as desks, a blackboard, and anti-Hitler posters that covered the union posters. The unpaid instructors were teachers of German from the high schools who came in their off-hours to teach the refugees. The system had its advantages: there was a variety of accents, a diversity of teaching methods, and amusement stemming from surprise. (Who will be teaching the course today? The little blond woman in glasses or the tall thin man with the crew-cut?) There were also some disadvantages: the cutting edge of the teaching sword, the lack of continuity in the coursework and the indecisiveness in the classes. Most of the volunteer teachers were communists or were sympathetic to communism. That was obvious from their choice of textbooks and their commentaries. Sometimes the classes went off onto impassioned tangents. While the teachers were mostly communist, not all the students were. Their ages ranged from Stefan's fourteen to the fifty and sixty of former engineers or researchers. It was there that Stefan learned what he could not very well have known as a child living in Germany: that German communists and their Social-Democratic *brothers* hated one another as much as they hated the Nazis. They accused one another of having made Hitler's bed for him. "From Noske to now, you've done nothing but shed communist blood!" cried the former. "In your hatred for the social-traitors, you have preferred to ally yourselves with the Nazis!" cried the

The Distant Friend

Socialists. Whenever the French class degenerated into such virulent historical and political discussions, Stefan stayed outside on the sidewalk of the Rue Lafayette listening as the groups continued to confront each other and trying to understand what the long quarrel was all about. Like a fire that would not go out, the conflict started up again at every turn of phrase and every change of wind. Stefan didn't know if he was more angry when the language lessons dissolved into long debates on political history or if he was more disillusioned when the lesson came to a stop in a discussion of the crimes of the social-fascists, traitors to the working class, or of the insanity of the Third International which had shortened the ladder Hitler climbed to power by lumping Socialists and Brown Shirts together.

While Ernst Friedrich was absent from Paris more and more frequently, Emma renewed contact with a branch of her family that she doubtlessly would not have continued seeing in Germany, because her "Aunt Esther," who was her first cousin, had long since allowed the Steins and Emma's parents to grow apart. For at least three generations, the Steins had become intellectuals or members of the professions, Good Germans even if they were suspect to the True Germans. Esther and her family had kept very much to Jewish ways. Whatever was the case with the branch that had stayed on in Germany, Esther had come to Paris to learn the Parisian costume jewelry business and had married Yankel, a Jew from Galicia, and had stayed in France. They spoke Yiddish among themselves, attended the synagogue, respected the ritual laws, and closed shop on Friday evening for the duration of the Sabbath. This way of life and doing things would have given Emma cold chills in Berlin in other times, the "better" times, but having found Esther again after months of solitude and inner torment in Paris, she now felt the protection of a home and the restful repose of tribal warmth. Esther took sincere pleasure in the return of her assimilated burgher cousin to traditional Jewish ways. It was a sort of victory of affection rather than of revenge, because there was nothing belligerent about Esther. Perhaps her only fault was that despite herself she reacted like a solid businesswoman, reasonable and shrewd. Her attachment to the family did not alter in any way the careful calculation of the salaries that she doled out to her relatives-employees.

When Stefan went to see his mother in the workrooms of Bijou-France, S.A., he was greeted by his cousin Esther, the family employees, and the employees-of-the-family as a child prodigy, the budding genius. He regarded their effusions and exclamations as an ethnographer observes the customary behavior of a tribal group he hardly knows. Nevertheless, it was cousin Esther who freed Stefan from living at the Gevaudeaus'. Despite the objections of his mother, whom the cousin managed to quiet down, Esther found a maid's room for him in the Rue Broulebarbe on the seventh floor, with water on the landing, a gas heater, a skylight looking out over the rooftops of the Latin Quarter, the stereotyped *vie de bohème,* you would say. At the age of fifteen, Stefan could not be a lodger in his own name, so Esther signed the lease for him and often lent him the money to pay the rent, which, however, was never given as a gift. Stefan bought some old shelves in the Flea Market for his books, and a basin of resonant zinc for his ablutions, and moved into his seven square meters. He looked at Paris through his skylight. As he had not yet read *Lost Illusions*, he did not cry out: "Here's to the two of us, Paris!"

Esther and her family were arrested by the French police in Nice in 1943 and turned over to the Germans. Not one of them returned from Auschwitz.

Stefan did all of the small and big jobs that a kid could get. Worse than that: a foreign kid. Worse than that: a German kid. Worse than that: a Jewish German kid. Worse than that: a kid who could be exploited with impunity. Compassion and gentle treatment generally amazed Stefan. In his eyes, the rule of thumb was to take advantage of him. He delivered his papers and worked as a sandwich man carrying signs that were too heavy for his meager shoulders. He replaced a neighboring janitor as furnace man for a building, was a packer at Sentier, and was acting interpreter in the summer for Cook Travel Agency. He read the Bible because he had been called a Jew. He read Marx because Hitler was against him. He went to the Sainte Geneviève Library because it closed late and he could read until ten o'clock at night. He filled notebooks with French words and idioms, with English vocabulary, and with quotations copied from the books he devoured. Once he had earned a bit of money, he divided it up into small packages made of newspaper, one packet for the rent, one for food, one for transportation, etc. He learned to go to the bakery and buy little bags of stale bread that could be made more edible by moistening it with water and passing it on the tongs of a fork over the gas flame. He bought the cheapest cuts of meat at the butcher's "for my cat," he said, to hide his shame. He found out that there were markets two or three times a week where you could buy vegetables that were no longer quite fresh and fruit that was bruised if you went just before closing time. But he took great care to avoid anything that might seem like a call for pity or, even worse than that, a kind of semi-beggary.

He washed his clothes with household soap in a small basin of enamelled zinc on the landing. Then he did the ironing with a cast-iron flatiron heated over the gas. He folded his only pair of pants under his mattress to keep the crease.

Sometimes he felt childish outbursts of violence erupting inside himself, a savage desire for a mouthful of chocolate which threw off the whole budget and the system of the packets of money. Or else he would watch the children play hopscotch, and once he understood the rules, he would return there at night to play by himself. A late passerby would have seen a thin, blond adolescent hopping around on the chalk on the sidewalk, somewhere between heaven and hell.

At sixteen, Stefan was leading the life of an ascetic, a veritable hermit living in Paris. The adolescent was a recluse one hundred years old. He had signed up for some correspondence courses. He got his first *bac* at the age of seventeen and his advanced diploma at eighteen. While he was waiting for the examining rooms to open, he watched the crowd of candidates, often accompanied by their parents or friends, comforting one another in their state of nervousness, all members of the great community of lycée, of coursework and companionship. As for Stefan, he was more the lone wolf of the comic strips of his childhood than ever, the *Lone Wolf,* the *Robin Hood of the West.* He had no biting envy, however, and felt no generalized resentment. All he wanted was to see the Nazis wiped out. In the newsreels, he saw Prime Minister Daladier on the Champs-Elysées, acclaimed for having signed the treaty with Hitler that turned Czechoslovakia over to Germany. "To know precisely who it is one hates," he was to say to me later on, "leaves plenty of room for kindness—or for indifference."

After two years of part-time jobs between a distant station and the Museum, the Professor finally got a permanent position at the Ornithological Station in Moustiers. The friendship of Lemire and the warm feelings of most of his French colleagues for him brought about the appointment to the position. To a certain extent, he could pursue his great work on acquired and innate behavior in ocean and swamp birds. He accumulated personal observations in the interludes between the modest functions that allowed him to eke out a living, counting the migratory birds, capturing and banding them, and inventorying the nests and eggs in the period of nesting. Neither anti-Semitism nor xenophobia had any adherents in his circles. On the contrary, Ernst Friedrich's colleagues who at first had organized the meritorious budgetary acrobatics to pay the Professor for his "vacations" had finally gotten decent compensation for him.

"I was sometimes able to tranform the bad times into the best luck in my life," Stefan told me the last time we were together. At the age of fourteen when he arrived in Paris,

torn from his native tongue, from his friends, from everything that had been life before that, discovering poverty
after an existence of ease, seeing his father constrained and
humiliated and his mother suddenly bent over, Stefan had
to face a double exile: he had been hounded from his
country and expelled forcibly from his childhood. He
bounced back, however.

Six years later his parents were still waiting for the much-
vaunted visa for the United States, which was slow in
coming, when suddenly the German-Soviet pact was
signed. Everyone near to them was certain that this meant
war. As soon as it began, all foreigners of "hostile na-
tionalities" would be interned in camps of the kind already
open in France for Spanish refugees from the Civil War and
other foreigners. They risked being caught between the
Nazi devil and the Russian blue sea. Professor Alvaro
Gutiérrez who, for two years, had been insisting that Stein
come to teach in Argentina at the university where he was
chancellor, sent a cablegram renewing his invitation and
including three passages on the SS *Christopher Columbus*
and the authorization to pick up three visas at the embassy
in Paris. The Professor would have preferred the United
States to Argentina. The ornithologists of the United
States are among the best in the world. Paterson, for example, knows all the birds of the world, and all the birds of five
continents know him. American laboratory equipment is
first-rate, but American bureaucracy, almost as sluggish in
its way as Soviet bureaucracy, could not make up its mind
whether to give the Steins the rubber stamp to go to New
York. They no longer had a choice. They were to embark

for Buenos Aires on September 28, 1939. Professor Stein made the trip to Paris to get the visas, and to confirm their passage on the *Christopher Columbus*. He also wanted to say goodbye to his French colleagues. The international news went from bad to worse. Stein came back on the twenty-third to get his family. He felt faint when he bent over to arrange some books in a valise. He was the first and only foreigner to be buried in our cemetery.

I remember making a kind of ridiculous statement to Stefan as we were standing on the station platform. "I will watch over your father's grave as if he had been my own."

That is how Stefan became the citizen of a South American country, something totally unexpected at the beginning of his destiny.

"So what?" he wrote to me in the first letter that got through to us thanks to the help of a Swiss diplomat, "a nationality is normally something you don't choose. You get it arbitrarily on arrival the way a harried warehouseman tosses a uniform to the distraught newcomer who has to do his best to fit into it. You're given a country without being asked your opinion. I did not choose this nation that has become my 'native land.' Would I have had any more reason to choose it if I had been born here? The nonsense on the brow of the executioner decreed that since I was born a Jew, I was a man without a country. The effect of that was to make of me . . . I won't say, like Goethe, a citizen of the world . . . that would be presumptuous. But perhaps a citizen of a place where people are not asked to be anything more than a citizen. . . ."

During his first visit to Breuil after the war in 1946, I

argued with Stefan that he was only twenty-six years old, t.
his naturalization papers were still pending and, as a consequence, he could still change direction, go back to his
point of departure and live in Germany again. He answered: no. He had received hospitality from Argentina in
a moment of great danger. He was able to pursue some very
difficult studies there. He would have considered it an act of
cowardice to leave once the storm had passed. His mother
had been greatly aged by her ordeals, and he could not see
moving her anywhere. As for returning to Germany, there
was no question of that; his feelings concerning his country
of birth were far too impassioned. Stefan felt that with
countries as with human beings, it is preferable, if possible,
to avoid the hot flames and their smoke (which he himself
did not always do). Between "the sacred love of the
Fatherland" or the love for a person, he preferred, as a rule,
loves of the heart and reason to volcanic loves. He felt a
cerebral attachment to his new country, and the feeling
that this land whose history and traditions were of short
duration, a land still in the process of formation, was the
beginning (or the re-beginning) that he needed so that he
himself could begin (or re-begin). And so he stayed there.

We were sometimes astonished by the fact that a man
who avoided idle conversation had chosen the profession of
lawyer whose objective should be justice, but whose raw
material is the word. Stefan answered that the profession
had chosen him rather than the other way around. He had
emigrated to this country that is called *new* because those
who populated it wiped out almost all trace of the original
inhabitants. Behind him he left an ancient nation where

ally abolished, where the "law of Nurem-
very word *law.*

ıt to leave Germany when Hitler, the
nor of the Third Reich, pronounced an important
speech at Leipzig before fourteen thousand German jurists.
Their spokesman had saluted Hitler saying: *"The fundamental law of the German people today is the will of the Führer."*

At the other extremity of Europe, the law did not seem
to be in any better shape during that same period. Stefan
had been struck by what happened to a Russian jurist of
Lithuanian origin whose name was Pachukanis. The latter
had published his *Theory of the Law's Decline* in Moscow in
1924. Thanks to the enlightenment of socialism, he en-
visaged the progressive and simultaneous extinction of the
law and of the state, as both were to become equally useless.
Pachukanis revised his thesis later on in his *Theory of the
Socialist State.* Vishinsky pointed out serious flaws in the
works. The debate took a less academic turn, and
Pachukanis was shot in 1936. The cement in the cellars of
Loubianka Prison was washed down after executions.

At the end of 1939, Stefan set out for a country where
law and rights were no more than words. If he had chosen
to begin law studies there, it was not with the idea of a
career in eloquence, but with the intention of dedicating
himself to the examination of the notion of justice. As a
lawyer, he was little inclined toward "results of the law
courts." More and more frequently, he laid aside his work at
the bar for his Chair in History and Philosophy of Law that
was offered to him several years later. He appreciated the
irony, as he put it, of "studying the history of law in a

country that has a short history, and that has little familiarity with the law."

In Breuil among my acquaintances, the word *law* only means disputes over field boundaries, squabbles over registries, or petty battles over inheritances. After the war when I received the first book that guaranteed Stefan an international reputation, *The State of the Law and the Law of the State*, I understood, given the context in which the book had been written and published, what the concept of law signifies. "You will see, when you finally give me the pleasure of coming to spend some time here," Stefan wrote to me, "that Europe has no monopoly on States without rights, without faith, and without law. . . ." (We had often talked about my projected trip to the Americas, but I am afraid that knowing myself and knowing life in Breuil with its rhythms of work and seasons, I will never make that crossing. . . .)

Specialists say that one of Stefan Stein's most original hypotheses in his philosophy of law is the theory of the Independent Arbitrator. *"Law,"* he says in the introduction to the book, *"not only implies a judge and those to be tried, but also an Independent Arbitrator, which fore-ordains Law in the name of Justice. The State always tends to combine the role of judge and Independent Arbitrator in a single function."* I don't feel sufficiently competent to judge the value of this theory. Not being a philosopher, I can only naively say that in conflicts between human beings, the only conceivable Independent Arbitrator would be a god external to humanity. And I don't think that is what Stefan means. . . . But what touches me personally, as in the less specialized essays that

Stefan published later on, is what surfaces of Stefan's life and of his own experiences and character. At the end of the first edition of *The State of the Law and the Law of the State*, Stefan wrote, *"The binder at the base of the hardened cement of States is more often blood than water."* I noticed that he eliminated those lines in the third edition. He explained to me that when he reread his work, he decided that his formula was only a commonplace decked out with a bit too much flashiness. As the years go by, Stefan tends more and more to lower the tone of his writings to let the ideas speak for themselves. He replaced his text by a poem written in youth by his childhood friend, Kurt Reichbach. Stefan and Kurt spent the summer of 1932 together in the Reichbach family chalet in the Black Forest in Germany. The two boys worked mornings on the balcony. The August sun accentuated a piercing odor of dry pine and turpentine. Kurt Reichbach's father, who had entered Dachau in October, 1939, died of typhus six days after the liberation of the camp. He had been denounced for having expressed doubts before witnesses about the official version of the burning of the Reichstag in February 1933. Kurt committed suicide in 1939.

·6·

I received a telegram dated from Boston from Stefan just a week after Mother's burial. His letter arrived five days after the telegram. I had had no news from him for some time. It is true that our friendship by the force of things and our circumstances had always been cut by long silences. My telegram had taken some time to reach him, as he was lecturing in the United States at Harvard, Yale, and Berkeley. He had resigned from his Chair on the faculty of the university in Buenos Aires after one of the innumerable military *coups d'état* that alternate regularly in Argentina with landslide electoral victories. If a democratic regime wins a victory, the army annuls the election as quickly as possible and takes power to see that the political opinion that has just been rejected by the voters will triumph. Stefan went back to his law office, but he is frequently called on to give lectures or seminars in American universities.

"You know what your mother meant to me," he wrote. "Losing her, forty years after the death of my father and twenty years after my own mother's, I have the feeling that the last line of defense that sheltered me, or that I thought was sheltering me, has gone.

"Until the day that we met each other on the La Conche beach, I always had the feeling that I was *on the other side of the door* in France. Sometimes the door was slammed in my face, sometimes I found it closed and didn't dare knock on it. At other times, it was ajar or even open, but I knew it was better not to try to cross the threshold. With you and with your mother, the door was wide open, and I walked in.

"You and I exchanged few words there on the beach during the first days of our acquaintance. You stayed in the background, less intimidated by me than 'snubbed' by your brother and Vincent. They wanted to talk German with me at all costs. Olivier had decided to show that he spoke it better than Vincent, and mercilessly corrected the latter's mistakes in declension. I can tell you now how much they exasperated me. I only wanted to talk French. To boot, both of them spoke a painfully labored classroom German. But your mother, who spoke no German at all, clearly saw through their game. She smiled mischievously at me when they squabbled over a point in grammar.

"But it was my first visit to Breuil after the vacation at Saint-Méjean when everything took shape. Your brother wasn't there. My father, your father, and my mother had begun to talk on the terrace under the wisteria. Your mother said, "Marie is late getting lunch ready. Would you excuse me ten minutes, Madame? . . . Come help me, boys." We followed her into the big kitchen where Marie was grumbling around the immense wood stove that still impresses me when I think about it. Your mother took up a basket of green beans and settled us around a table in the pantry, and she laughed because I had never cut string beans before. She showed me how to do it, a quick snap at the top and another at the bottom, then toss the string into an old newspaper and the beans into a salad bowl. We went happily about the business of stringing green beans. Your mother babbled on *incoherently* (that's how I thought you said what I wanted to express in French, even confusing it with *at once*) and *by fits and stops.* You dared tell me that the correct expression was *by fits and starts* only when we were alone together, and your thoughtfulness touched me. (When your brother corrected my French, he did so with such seriousness and fanfare that everyone felt that he was modestly fulfilling an obligation of hospitality and assistance, and that I should be grateful to him for his attention and his pedagogical patience.) My own mother, who very quickly found herself alienated from the conversation of the two men who got into the subject of "their" wars all over again, and who had not very well understood what had happened when your mother had vanished with us, came to join us and asked to help with the green-bean operation. Everything was suddenly so simple, so amicable and so *obvious* in our group sitting around the round table pulling out the little fresh brittle green stems, that I felt as though I had been totally adopted by a real family. I was no longer an outsider, but one of you. I'm undoubtedly going to make you smile, but whenever anyone serves me green beans now, they have the effect of Proust's madeleine, and I see your mother once again, the blue apron she had put on over her summer dress, her smile, and I hear the conversation *by fits and stops,* and my heart is full."

After lunch was over and the grownups were having coffee, my mother had said to me: "Etienne, you should take Stefan and show him around the house and property," and off we went, the two of us. I took Stefan into the barns, the stables, the sheds, the winepress, the washrooms, and the winecellars, and then I took him through the house, from the bedrooms up to the attic and back down to my room. He looked at the books I had arranged in the circular bookcase at the head of my bed and said to me: "So you cover your books with transparent paper too?" "The ones I like best," I answered. He said: "Then I'll know which ones you like best," and I blushed. He ran a finger the length of the sage and shining books in their Sunday best, their transparent covers . . . "Baudelaire . . . Rimbaud . . . Verlaine . . . Auguste Angellier . . . Balzac . . . *Dominique* . . . *Le Grand Meaulnes* . . . Charles Morgan . . ." He did not know the latter. I said: "He's an important English writer. It's a beautiful book. I'll lend it to you if you like. . . ." Then, since we'd been using the formal "vous" form of address, I asked him: "Can we use 'tu' with each other?" and I was a bit embarrassed because as I said that I sort of choked up. Stefan answered, using the "tu" form to me: "I can lend you some books too, if you want. I have quite a few in French, mostly in Paris, but I can show you the ones I have in Moustiers."

From that day on, we have always used the familiar "tu" form of address with each other.

As I was expecting someone to come looking for us to have a bit of supper and as I wanted to "keep Stefan to myself," because up to that time I had never been with him by myself, I suggested we take a walk through the woods, and he agreed. I can't remember our conversation any more today except for the music and not the words, and except for the happiness we felt at being together, and at being able to explore each other, compare our thoughts, and take each other's measure, to talk of our treasures, the poets we loved, the musicians we knew, what (little) we had seen of art, just as two small children pour their toys out on the table like a gift to be shared. It seemed to me that what I was feeling was something I had never felt before; I finally had someone with whom I could share my thoughts, which just went to prove that I had some thoughts. At home my opinion was rarely asked, and from the beginning I became accustomed to keeping my opinions to myself. As it seemed to me that my opinions were of no interest to anyone and that no one really took me seriously, I came to the point of having no opinions about anything and of leaving those ideas of mine that no one ever asked about in a kind of hazy blur. When he gave me his friendship, Stefan suddenly bestowed on me an importance that I had never recognized in myself.

At the end of that day when the time came to accompany the Steins to the station for the local train that was to take them back to Moustiers, I was filled with despair. I had just *found* Stefan, and was losing him already! While my parents and his stood chatting on the station platform, Stefan and I exchanged the promise never to lose sight of each other. How could we keep that promise? Stefan would be free only until he enrolled in the university, which was a month and a half away. Moustiers was quite a long distance from Breuil. Consequently, he could come to visit at Christmas, Easter, and during summer vacation. An interminable stretch of absences and separations was ahead of us. . . .

Friendship's passion, that joyous movement of the spirit and the blood that animated me, the desire to talk with Stefan, to be with him and to verify myself through him, drove me to acts which I would have thought myself incapable of doing. I did not request, I *demanded* a motorbike. The tone I took to explain this desire was something that left Mother flabbergasted, and my father quieter than ever. I pointed out with vehemence that it was impossible to oversee the operations of the property without that work instrument, that I lost excessive amounts of time going from one field to the other or from one vineyard to another on the farm. I was listened to and got approval, my wish fulfilled. The confidence that Stefan accorded me inspired a confidence in its turn that I rarely felt otherwise. As soon as I had the motorbike, I was off on the road to Moustiers as often as Stefan took the one toward Breuil.

Now when I recall that year, I recognize that it was a dark year. War was approaching, gathering overhead like a storm either about to burst or to hold off for a while, moving away, then coming back to break upon us. The Steins were waiting for the visa that would allow them to leave Europe. I was torn between wanting Stefan to be able to go away, and the feeling of sadness that if he emigrated, I would lose him. He was doubly precious to me: because he was there, my witness. Because he might not be there any longer one day soon, my lost friend.

Today Stefan is that long gentleman looking wholly Anglo-Saxon, tall, very thin, his forehead high, blond hair tending toward white, his blue eyes behind steel glasses as before, unfolding his long legs and long arms like a very lean insect. I once said to him: "You have really become Steven Sting . . . the American." He laughed. At that time, he was blond, tanned, and athletic. My brother said: "Stefan has that extraordinary beauty of the Jews of Europe who resemble Siegfried or Parsifal, just as the Jews of the Orient resemble an Arab sheik and, as they age, an old mufti." Julie simply said: "Stefan is divine." She managed to pass through Breuil "accidentally" on the days he came to see me. He treated her with a playful and meticulous courtesy that exasperated poor Julie. We learned that when the university at Poitiers reopened she had registered for work toward a *licence* in English. No one was fooled by her new vocation. It only lasted two weeks. Vincent explained to me: "My sister was talking about doing work in English, but I think she was more inclined toward German. It must not have worked out, because here she is with her studies over before they even started." I have often wondered what happened, if Julie had "conquered" Stefan and then quickly lost him, or if he had rejected her and, in either case, if Stefan had guessed that I was not insensitive to Julie's acidity and had cut things off *because of me and because of him.*

What could Stefan find to like in me? I've asked myself

that many times. I sometimes told myself that it was not my character or the personality that I feared I lacked, but my situation. When he came back to Europe after the war in 1946, he said to me: "I was afraid everything would be changed. I find you all just the same." "Alas!" I answered.

"You don't know how lucky you are," he said. "You have what is denied me. There isn't a piece of furniture that you use or an object that you touch, not a table, not a wardrobe, not a single spoon or hairbrush that doesn't have a history that is part of the history of your family."

That was true, and returning to Breuil was like finding oneself again, just as you find your comfortable spot on the sofa that is battered and lumpy from years of use, but whose hollows and humps give the impression, however illusory, of constancy.

In the living room at Breuil, the clock with the slender Doric oak columns, its sluggish copper pendulum, and its globe for a bridal wreath still loses five minutes a day after fifty years despite five or six useless repairs by the clockmaker. Stefan liked to make comments about it whenever he was present at what he called "the ceremony of resetting the clock," a ceremony at which I always officiated (and still do). As I never could remember whether two or three or four days had passed since I had reset the hands, and whether I had to move them ahead five or ten or fifteen minutes, and as no one in the house had a watch showing the same time, there were all sorts of laughs and jokes until my brother would decide to phone for the recorded time. The last time Stefan was in Breuil after our first dinner together, I gave him the pleasure of the immutable ceremony of the resetting of the clock while we were having coffee.

"It is a symbol of your country," Stefan said. "It tries to be on time with the world, but—I want to say: happily—it does so only with difficulty. Being on time with the world signifies that nomadism of wholly modern countries, far more nomadic than the ancient nomads of the deserts or of shepherds with their movements to and from winter and spring pastures. It signifies America where almost everyone moves from one end of the continent to the other several times in a lifetime, whereas after three centuries a house like yours deserves to be called a *home,* that beautiful word that only I really pay attention to, no doubt because I am a foreigner and have been forced to be a nomad. How I would like to *be at home* somewhere. . . ." I answered that in the Midi region, a *homebody* was considered to be someone who was slightly retarded, backward, and somewhat deficient. I still wonder if, by dint of living in a single dwelling, I have not become a *homebody* in the sense of the definition above. . . . We argued the matter at some length. Is it good to stay in the same place, to put down deep roots and submerge oneself in memories? On the other hand, must one always be prepared to depart, to be receptive and open to every opportunity, to be free? That debate has been going on for seventy years or more. It was the subject of a quarrel between two writers, the aged Maurice Barrès and the young André Gide, a debate over land and the dead. "We Jews," said Stefan, "no longer have land, but we have the dead."

But at the same time that he partially based his pleasure

in coming back to Breuil and his friendship for me on the stability of the family and the house as well as on the certainty that he would find us still in the same old place, Stefan could also get carried away at times and try to cure me forcibly of what the moment before had pleased him so. "I can't stand the way you accept everything that happens to you, the mean tricks played on you or the evil done to you without a word of protest, even almost with a sort of covert pleasure. It's shameful, yes," he repeated, "shameful!"

When he came back in 1946, I told him the story of *my war*.

After what we called the *funny war*, the uneventful months before the German invasion when I had been declared unfit for service because of a hernia, the underground Resistance fighters had come to me to ask for help. In 1941, at the beginning of the Nazi occupation, the Resistance consisted of a dozen persons in our canton who did not agree with either the Germans or the Vichy government of Marshal Pétain. One man named Pique-Chidouille hid anti-German tracts and small posters in the vault of the Lecène-Mancheron family whose head was the president of the local *Légion des Combattants*. The Marshal had warmly shaken Lecène-Mancheron's hand when the "Head of State" had come to visit Poitiers. I gave shelter in Breuil to the antiquated mimeograph machine of the forbidden *Union des Syndicats*. I later learned that the communist Micheau had stashed it with me because Claveau, an employee of the Farmers' Credit Union, and Gendron, the hardware dealer, had wanted to take it for use by a rival group. They had actually set up a network called "Honor to the Homeland," a network that was politically to the right of the communists and their allies, a movement that was no less patriotically entitled "Forward France!" (and below it: "Out with the Krauts!").

As I was tired of the underhanded dealings and the ridiculous bickering between the adherents of "Honor to the Homeland" and "Forward France," I decided to help a friend of Vincent's whom the latter had sent to me. Vincent had organized an escape network for Allied pilots shot down over France and for escaped Anglo-Saxon prisoners. There was a series of relays through which they were passed as far as the Spanish border where smugglers got them across the frontier. For a year and a half, we regularly sheltered English and American aviators. Stefan lost his temper when I laughingly told him how the regional delegate of the network had announced to me that only four medals of the Resistance were to be awarded to our unit, and that one had already been assigned posthumously to a comrade who had been arrested and deported, and who had died in a camp in Germany, and three comrades who were government employees who would have far more need of the citation for their pensions and retirement benefits than I would as working farmer. "It's a disgrace," said Stefan. "You stick out your cheek so they can strike you. . . . You want me to tell you something? To me, a Jew, you represent what I detest in some Jews, a mixture of ridiculous resignation and humility, of masochistic humor, and of simple-minded other-worldliness, all of which makes me vomit. I have troubling reservations about Zionism, and I am not certain that having a land of one's own is recompense for the inconvenience of being represented by a State. . . . But after Auschwitz and Treblinka, when I see a young Jew standing holding a machine gun even if externally and superficially he has a certain resemblance to a young Fascist, it makes me damned happy. . . . But you, you with your way of making excuses for being the person you are, to joke about the filthy tricks they pull on you, to find it normal for your brother to always take the best portions and leave you the leftovers, to always say yes when someone 'suggests' an order and 'thank you' when you've been treated rottenly, do you want to know how I feel about that? You disgust me, Etienne, you disgust me!"

And as I knew that that was not true, and that it could well be that I was installed once and for all in the comfortable fortress of masochism, when Stefan got so worked up and had gruffly showered me with insults, I was deeply happy. His anger was proof of his affection.

Nevertheless, he was unable to convince me that I was wrong in being *submissive,* as he put it, and in not rebelling. All I need is a look at Stefan to wipe out the very thought of complaining. "Why him and not me?" It's no use for him to repeat to me that nothing is more unhealthy than to feel guilt for having been spared from misfortune, and the bad conscience of the survivor is inspired by the Devil or his modern equivalent, the instinct for death, and so I never feel quite well adjusted.

Stefan says that I have all the vices of a Christian without having the virtues, that I turn the other cheek to the would-be striker without really forgiving, and that I have the weaknesses of Jews, but not their pride. "What you lack, Etienne, is true *meanness*, a healthy maliciousness, and having a little stubborn evil in you to combat evil." I know very well that my life has been protected from the wounds that have marked Stefan. I have experienced nothing, or very little, of what he has undergone. I have never made anyone submit to what men have made him go through. Perhaps I should say: I have never had to go through. . . . I have never had to make anyone else go through. . . . The question that I constantly ask myself is, I know, a vain one. If fate had made it my lot to be a victim, how would I have behaved? If I had chosen by destiny to be sent off with the torturers, would I have had the strength to hold out against them? The other day I found an image in an old Elizabethan drama that set me to thinking: *"Man is like a dungheap: you have to crush it to know its odor."* I have never been crushed. Stefan has been. I don't know what my odor is like. We do know what Stefan's is like.

He is wrong, however, to consider me otherworldly and to think that I see the world through rose-colored glasses. I was thinking about that yesterday as I came home from the cemetery where I had to pay Pique-Chidouille. I strolled among the tombs for quite a while. I went all the way to the wall down below, as far as the little gateway that opens onto the stream that separates the cemetery from the fields. Sometimes, given my propensity for lugubrious irony, I tell myself that I lived some of the happiest hours of my childhood in this cemetery. But they were no more than days of quiet between savage games. I even tell myself that we were like little animals whose parents prepare and train them for the hunt awaiting them, the kittens taught by their mother to pounce on their prey. At home everyone asked, "Where could that child have gone to now?"

That particular year, I was constantly at the cemetery. But who would have thought to look for me there? On weekdays when the school year was over, that was where I found quiet, in Monsieur Labeur's cabin, or down below on the other side of the gate that was closed at night. That gate is right by the wooden footbridge over the stream bordered by alders and willows in the middle of a great field of poplars. Monsieur Labeur was the husband of Louisa La- beur, my parents' laundress. Monsieur Labeur was the equivalent, with a great deal more dignity, of his successor at the cemetery, the man who had been his lieutenant, Pique-Chidouille. Monsieur Labeur was a man of all trades: guardian, gravedigger, gardener, something of a mason, and something of a stonecutter, in addition to the unexpected things that came up constantly, like repairing the walls of the tombs, fixing the bolts of the vaults, and arranging the plants and cuttings of the new burials as well as of the older family vaults. Monsieur Labeur and Pique-Chidouille also had their vegetable garden in the field that ajoins the cemetery down below. It required constant care. Monsieur Labeur worked there from early morning until sundown. The days are very long in the summertime.

We would play a game called Wars of Catholics against Protestants in the schoolyard until time for the distribution of prizes. There was quite a choice of other wars. There was the Great War of 1914–1918, of course, and cowboys and Indians, and the Moroccan leader Abd el-Krim against the

French. Real wars often take place the way play wars do. You start by declaring war, then you find a reason for waging it. We fought at school for the pleasure of fighting. That year, the "reason" that we found, after the blows had started to fall, was the history lesson taught by Monsieur Cauvin who was the regular teacher, and the Elementary Course written by Ernest Lavisse of the French Academy. There are still Protestants and Catholics in my country. They have not made war on one another for a long time, but their graves are separated. In other eras, the Huguenots were allowed to bury their dead on the land of their own property. When you see a cypress somewhere away from a house either near a wine cellar or an orchard, you know that it's the grave of a Protestant. Even today, the Protestants are on one side of the cemetery and the Catholics on the other. And while they are alive, the latter go to mass on Sunday and to catechism, and the former to church and to Sunday School. As for the rest, there are neither differences nor disputes. But Monsieur Ernest Lavisse reminds us that "*in the time of King Francis the First in the sixteenth century, some Frenchmen did not want to remain Catholic and converted to Protestantism. The Catholics detested the Protestants, and the Protestants detested the Catholics. They did a great deal of harm to one another.*" The fact that the Queen Mother, Catherine de Medici, was "*an evil woman*" sufficed to bring about the Saint Bartholomew's Day massacre. "*The murderers went into the house of the Protestant leader Coligny and found him sleeping. They struck him with their swords and threw him out of the upstairs window. Here you see him. He died from the fall.*"

91

In one of his last books, *The Politics of the Tabula Rasa*, Stefan wrote that if our own century had to choose a patron saint, it would be Saint Bartholomew without doubt whatsoever. "*He was, moreover, a very gentle man,*" he says. "*We know very little about him except that he walked from his native Galilee as far as India to teach a Hebrew gospel to the Indians. The irony of history is that the name of this peaceful man is associated with a famous political massacre, even though today it seems like a modest affair: we have done much better at killing since then.*"

When we children would play Saint Bartholomew's Day, it was usually little Rapeneau, the son of the Widow Rapeneau, who was chosen by common consent to take the part of Admiral Coligny. As we could not hang him from a window sill and then have him fall, we just drowned him instead. Lattrape and Coupeau would stick his head down into the barrel of soft water where the rain runs down the gutter of the blacksmith's shop next to the Church Square. Lattrape would hold his hands, and Coupeau would stick his head in. Little Rapeneau may not have been very strong, but he could kick like a mule. But if he was held under water long enough, he got tired and wasn't dangerous any more. All the same, it was better to pull him out of the tub before he really drowned.

Rapeneau really was a Protestant, but in the two armies, the Catholic and the Protestant, things were not so simple. Big Fillioux had pointed out that if the Catholics were all real ones in the war, and if the Protestants were real ones too, there wouldn't be any more game because it would no longer be a game. We had to draw lots so that we would all be mixed up, and the real Protestants could wage war as false Catholics, and the Catholics could fight as Protestants. At any rate, you play a game to have a good time, and even if you do some harm, it's not for real. The important thing is to have two armies that can wage war.

Admiral Coligny was standing near the tub, streaming with water, coughing-crying-spitting, with his ears still buzzing. The Widow Rapeneau came out of the washhouse with her wooden wash paddle in her hand, her clogs click-clacking on the pavement. "Just what have you been up to now? There, take that, that will teach you to bedevil your poor mother." Now Admiral Coligny really had something to cry about.

The Huguenots formed an advance party to scout the road leading from the tanneries to the communal washhouse. When they fanned out into the Church Square, the Catholics were lying in ambush behind the plane trees. The fire nourished by automatic arms and the cry repeated a thousand times over (in the accounts of battles, the battle cries are always repeated a-thousand-times-over), and the cry repeated a-thousand-times-over of *"Protestinkers! Protestinkers!"* cut their momentum short. They hesitated for a moment. There was a wavering in their deployment, but the enemy wasn't quick enough to take advantage of it. But the Huguenots caught sight of Lattrape and Coupeau, who were moving in open terrain. Gatereau, the Protestant general, took advantage of surprise. "Forward! Charge!" And the Huguenots made a rush at the two loners, who couldn't make up their minds whether to fall straight back from where they were, in danger of being totally cut off from their comrades, or to make a foolhardy attempt, under the very nose of the enemy, at joining the main body of the Catholics who were hidden behind the trunks of the trees. They tried to rejoin the others by a detour, and that was what brought about their defeat, along with their friends'. Gatereau and his friends behind him attacked, cutting the Catholics into two sections, one of which had tried to come to the aid of the two boys. There was a general free-for-all, the Huguenots took one prisoner, Mathiard, and all we had to do then was to go off, one of the troops straight to the cemetery, and the other behind the church to go around to the entrance. In the breathless confusion and crunching of hob-nailed shoes, one clogwearer suddenly took off his wooden shoes and carried them in his hands, while clods of earth rained down on the combatants.

Since the Catholics had gone into the cemetery, Gatereau brought his troops to a halt.

"No kidding. They're lousy enough to ambush us. . . . Where is the prisoner?"

"Here, Captain."

The prisoner was bound with a leather belt. Nothing to be proud of.

"And now, you guys, we'll get them! You over there, stay here and guard the gate. Get behind the entrance. The rest of us will go down the big lane, we'll roust them out and bring them back here, and then we all fall on them at the same time."

The main walkway was the one with the beautiful family vaults with wrought-iron grilles, marble slabs, angels of real stone, gilded vases, real flowers, wreaths of wire, and all in natural colors.

The Protestant army was coming down the central path with stealthy tread, looking around to be sure that there weren't any infiltrations from the lateral lanes, but Monsieur Labeur suddenly loomed up in front of them thundering: "Who in the devil stuck me with these dirty little brats who think my cemetery is a circus! You're going to get out of here right now, and the faster the better!" The men of both armies sheepishly beat a fast retreat toward the exit with a furious Monsieur Labeur on their heels shouting as he let them go through the gate: "And I better not catch you in here again, or else!"

It was a long time before anyone saw the invaders playing war games in the cemetery again. Monsieur Labeur reigned over peace and quiet once more. He was tall and thin, with wrinkles up and down his face and a salt-and-pepper mustache crosswise, always wearing a carpenter's cap on his head, and a blue flannel belt over trousers with the kind of tight-fitting legs nobody wears any more. He seldom spoke, but was always very precise when he did. We had become friends the day that Monsieur Labeur had snatched me from the clutches of big Malbec and Sonchamps in front of the church. The latter had decided to relieve me of my agate marbles and a Swiss pocket-knife I had just been given as a present. I was smaller than they and a lot less strong. I was about to give in when Monsieur Labeur, who was wheeling some compost toward the cemetery, saw what was happening, dropped the handles of his barrow, and stepped in. He took the marbles and the Swiss knife back from the extortioners and handed them to me, then he watched in silence as the crooks took off. "If they bother you again, come see me. I'll show you where I work."

For Monsieur Labeur the work with the dead was clear, orderly, and quiet. His tool shed was always very neat, freshly swept, and with the tools hung in order along the wooden wall. He had used thumbtacks to stick on another wall some pictures cut out of old calendars, pictures of swans on a blue lake at sunset, a family of blue-point kittens looking at an object, and a squirrel in autumn fur against a background of golden leaves. He made temporary crosses out of wood, regilded the inscriptions of letters that had washed away or worn away on the marble slabs, used a soldering iron to repair a section of a grille that was damaged, reattached hinges, and polished marble. His shed smelled of sawdust, fresh earth, and heated metal. Among his graves, his tombs, and his vaults, Monsieur Labeur was tidy, calm, and precise, an efficient master of the passenger station of the dead. His assistant had less class. In the stream that flows on the other side of the cemetery wall, down below, Pique-Chidouille always had a bottle cooling. On the other bank by the wooden footbridge, Pique-Chidouille had his vegetable garden. Soil near the dead produces first-rate vegetables.

On weekdays during my childhood when there were no children running around playing a game of war, the cemetery was certainly the quietest place in all of our little town. There were visitors only on Sunday and on All Saints' Day, or else very early in the morning, just after mass, when two piously faithful widows tidied up the graves of two dearly departed spouses, first pulling up a weed here and then taking out a woolen handkerchief to dust off a porcelain plaque containing the portrait of the mustachioed dead man photographed full-face.

When the distribution of school prizes was over, I often would sneak out of the house. I left my brother and my cousins and the neighborhood children to their busy games, and I would slip into the cemetery taking care to be seen by no one. Monsieur Labeur had made me a fishing pole that he put away in his shed. I would cruelly thread half an earthworm onto the hook and then go toss the line into the stream. Big blue dragonflies with compound eyes would land on the pole. I could see minnows and roaches wriggling in the current, but I never caught any. Then I would go daydream or nap under the willows and alders that grew along the riverbank.

At the end of the summer the year before I got my diploma, Monsieur Labeur was going through agony. Monsieur Arnoud, the bailiff, and Monsieur Labat, the teacher-secretary of the town hall, both of whom were in charge of the Archeological Society of which I now, forty-five years later, am president, had brought Monsieur Labeur a large box of white wood that he had carefully placed in a corner of his shed. "Don't you touch that," he said to me. I was intrigued by the box. To have some peace and to show me that curiosity is an ugly defect and that such satisfaction is its own punishment, Monsieur Labeur abruptly opened the box. It was full of tibias, femurs, and skulls. I was a lot less frightened than Monsieur Labeur had expected. Those old bones, so carefully arranged, were like the ones Monsieur Labat showed us at school when we studied anatomy, rather like practice study materials. "You see there, you little scamp, I don't know what to do with what's left of those Christians there. What kind of Christians could they be? Monsieur Arnoud and Monsieur Labat had a funny idea to go digging around over there at Arpaillac, where there was once a big battle between the Protestants and the Catholics. They found these old bones there, and they want me to bury them. But where? With the Prots or with the Catholics? That's a devil of a situation to put me in! What would you do in my place, you little scamp?"

After giving it much thought, Monsieur Labeur buried the "archeological" bones in the common grave that is against the lower wall with more recent remains (if one can call them that), the bones from tombs that were abandoned and had had no one come to care for them in dozens of years. "That way they'll all be together," said Monsieur Labeur, "the good Christians, the Protestinkers, the ones that don't go to mass, the ones who died on the field of honor, and the ones who died in their beds. What do you want, you little scamp, it all ends up that way, and the cemetery's the only spot I know where I don't see any fights."

Today as I stroll through the old cemetery, I can still hear the gusts of the past with their cries of childhood, the imprecations of the stage setting of our transformation of a game of religious wars that were extinguished here only to burst out elsewhere. Sometimes it seems to me that the warlike games of my childhood, the archives of our past, and the memories of the Nazi Occupation all persist in telling the same story, *"a tale told by an idiot, full of sound and fury."* During the Revolution, it was on the borders of our province, in Vendée, that the Blues, partisans of the Republic, filled wells with the cadavers of the Whites, who were Royalists, or ripped open the stomach of one of the women followers of the leader Jean Chouan, with a bayonet, and then stuffed it with straw. At about the same time, at Nantes, Jean Baptiste Carrier drowned the enemies of the Republic by the hundreds. That was the day before yesterday. Before that (1542), a young man's tongue was cut out for saying offensive things about miraculous images and having maintained that they barely differed from the stone gods of the pagans. That Protestant youth of nineteen years stuck his tongue out to the executioner who pulled it out as far as possible with a pair of pincers, cut it off, and then struck the heretic three times on the cheek before taking him off to be burned at the stake.

In 1944 I took the Limoges-Angoulême-Paris road with Colonel Bayard, the head of the Maquis underground fighters. He had a meticulous memory of graves. The road was lined wth them: militiamen, collaborators with the Germans, or people suspected of being collaborators. "That's where that bastard was shot. . . . This is where So-and-So was executed." Colonel Bayard was a brave man determined to "build a socialist society," and a bit sentimental. He had just been present at the exhumation of the bodies of three young people of our little town. In December of 1943, the Germans had tortured them at length with blowtorches. In 1562 the turncoat, Baron Adrets, explained to the writer

D'Aubigné that it was necessary to watch Huguenot women and children die without feeling any pity. That very morning he had just returned to the enemy three hundred horsemen loaded onto chariots, each one with a foot and a hand cut off. In fundamentalist Islamic countries today, thieves' hands are cut off (under medical supervision, of course). And the Imam Khomeini sends schoolboys off to war. But just yesterday in our own country, the Great Condé recounted how the nobleman Joachim de Bois-Jourdan, after killing the Huguenot Jean de la Noue with his own hand, had his nephew, aged fourteen or fifteen, strike the corpse in the stomach with a dagger "to accustom the boy to blood and killing." Given such things as that, what is surprising about an eyewitness saying that on Saint Bartholomew's Day *"the blood flowed in the streets as though there had been a heavy rain"?*

· 7 ·

Fifty years is quite a bit of time. A half-century is already History. I prefer to say that I have known Stefan for forty-eight years. We renewed ties fairly frequently during those years, but at intervals that were sufficiently long for us to see with a clear eye how we were aging. In the house in Breuil there is a doorway to the dining room where Mother used to measure Olivier and me over the years, marking Olivier's height on the doorframe with a red pencil, and mine with blue. When Olivier and I stopped growing, those measurements came to signify the visits that Stefan made. When I saw him again and noticed how much thinner he was getting, a bit askew in his bulky carcass but not yet stooped over despite the look of his shoulders announcing that that would not be long in coming, I often saw myself through other eyes. I had paid little attention to the ravages of time on myself, but when they touched my friend, I became conscious of them.

I said that each time we got together again, we quickly renewed the ties of friendship, but I am not sure that I am not getting ahead of my story. I take pride, perhaps wrongly, in thinking that Stefan is my friend, my *best friend*. I know very well that there's something puerile in wanting at any price to establish a classification of one's affections. When I say that Stefan is my *best friend*, I have the impression of going back to grade school when we chose a *best friend*, and when we swore to remain friends, *best friends* for all our lives. It is because I know that Stefan is in contact with people who are so much more intelligent and important than I, people who are his equals, his peers, persons of distinction next to whom I am a nobody. But I flatter myself sometimes that the attachment to me that he shows is of another kind. And when I go off on a tangent, I even go so far as to tell myself that he cares for the others for what they do, but that he cares for me, a nobody, for what I am. Does he return to Breuil as one hastens to an interlocutor, an equal? Or does he come back here to us as one immerses oneself in a home? We are the family he no longer has. I am the relative he has not lost, the brother that he never had, one of his cousins who did not disappear in the camps or was not swallowed up in exile. Does one feel friendship for a relative? Perhaps sometimes. But more often one feels affection, or gets into a habit, or acts through the accumulation of time. Friendship is something else. And once I had reflected on these things for some time, I came to the conclusion that Stefan is not my best friend, but something different—a member of the family. . . .

If he were to hear me speak that way, Stefan would surely tell me that it is my undue humility that causes me to think that way. But Stefan's life is richer and more varied than mine. What he writes, his thinking, becomes more and more difficult for me to understand. I have such a time following his books and assimilating them that I don't dare speak of his works while he is here. During our long separations, I read his books and take notes on them. I make up a list of questions that I intend to ask him when we are together again. Then when he's here, I haven't the courage to ask them. We talk about other things, his new country, for example. I wouldn't venture to call it his adopted country because deep down Stefan has only adopted Argentina through a decree of the spirit. I am not certain that Argentina has adopted Stefan, despite the renown that he has acquired, some of which brings honor to the country where he is living and working. But as he says himself, it is in the United States and in Europe that his name is becoming well known. He became recognized in Buenos Aires through a sort of echo and undertow, when voices from abroad began to spread his name as an exceptional historian and philosopher. Stefan says that it is difficult to imagine the contradictions and contrasts in the country where fate "dropped" him. "I left Nazi Germany," he said, "only to find myself in a country where an important segment of the nation was wishing for a Hitler victory, and where the working class acclaimed a populist-fascist *caudillo*, and made a cult of the Madonna of dubious background and origins who was his wife. A country where the best and the worst of Europe are joined." Then he added: "I have become an intellectual in a land where the slogan of the

Peronists was 'Long live espadrilles! Down with books!' I took shelter from anti-Semitism in a country where anti-Semitism is as common as horseflies on cattle."

He also says that there is a certain black humor in having become a specialist in the history of law on that side of the Atlantic where law is less widespread as a notion than macho virility and its symbols—the knife, the pistol, the lasso and spurs. "But I'm being unjust," he added. "If you consider the ensemble of the European continent, law is only even nominally respected in very few nations. If you go deeply into time or space to try to write a history of the development of law, you write the history of gossamer threads hovering above an immense forest. Fifty years ago in Frankfurt, chains that locked the Jews into their ghetto for the night were attached to the boundary stones every evening. When it was promulgated, the Constitution of the United States of America stipulated that a Negro would be counted in the census as representing only three-fifths of an inhabitant. The Nuremberg laws had deep roots which were not all German. . . ."

For quite some time I thought that Stefan's friendship had dissipated. He had come back to Europe a year and a half after the end of World War II, in 1946. He had avoided returning to Germany, but after he had taken care of matters in Paris, he came to Breuil, and we spent a week listening to his stories about life in Argentina, and to his questions about the Nazi Occupation of France. We had truly found each other once again, and the thick layers of the dark years that had flowed by since our separation in 1939 did not prevent us from seeing the clarity of the days of our youth intact, as if through the glaze on a painting. A long absence followed that visit. I wrote to Stefan, but I had the feeling that my letters could not be of interest to him. The chores of taking care of the property, Mother's health, the condition of the harvest, Olivier's career, Pinay's loan, my reading—what did I have to tell Stefan that really concerned him? On the other hand, those years for him were very productive ones. He had begun by working in a lawyer's office. He said that the profession intrigued him because it put him in contact with the real life of real people. Later on, when he had become famous through his books, during the several years that he occupied the Chair of the History of Law and before he resigned at the time of one of the periodic returns of the military to power, he always refused to stop taking court cases. He said that to stop would be like a doctor doing research who would refuse to have any contact with his patients. "I am not purely a laboratory man," he said.

I had set myself to learning Spanish so that I could follow Stefan's work. He was touched when I asked him to send me copies of his publications. He had commented that most of his writings were published in Spanish. I was able to answer him that now I could read Spanish. "I hope I never have to emigrate again in my lifetime and learn to speak a fifth language," he wrote to me. "I can picture you trying to follow me and working evenings at Breuil to learn Lapp or Swahili. . . ."

It seemed to me, however, that we were losing contact with each other during those years. His letters were infrequent and impersonal, like information bulletins. The tone became warmer, as was natural, when, a few months later, Stefan's mother died, then my father. Madame Stein had made herself a kind of German life in exile, Stefan told me. She had become reacquainted with some distant relatives, had made friends, went to the synagogue, and almost succeeded in forgetting that she was in Latin America living in a German-Jewish bubble. My father had become increasingly taciturn, and silence finally completely engulfed him.

Then Stefan seemed to distance himself once more, until the day that the great news came to us: Stefan was going to get married. A month later he was crowned by one of the most important prizes awarded in Germany, the Minerva Prize, and he had agreed to go to Frankfurt to receive it. He told us that he would come to Breuil on his return trip to introduce his wife to us, if that was agreeable.

Nora was American, from an old Vermont family that had looked with jaundiced eye on Eleanor McInes's marriage to a Jew of questionable identity: German by birth, Hispano–Anglo-Saxon–French by culture, South American by nationality, cosmopolitan by fame, lawyer and professor of law, an author of boring books, and clearly without money.

The announcement of Stefan's visit with his new wife provoked an unprecedented stir in the household at Breuil. Madame Lhoumeau, who had once taken a tour to the United States, had pointed out that all Anglo-Saxons slept in twin beds, rather than the double vessels of mahogany larded with bolsters, padded with pillows, and gleaming with the red down comforters we use in France. The whole house was ransacked for three days while a search went on to find two twin beds for the big bedroom, two beds that were not exactly twin because they were not the same age, one being the small divan that had been brought up from the rose salon and the other, a teenager's bed carried down from the attic. Marquette the plumber was summoned in haste and put to work right away refurbishing the bathrooms, which required changing the bathtub, whose enamel had become crazed, tarnished and slightly blackened with the years. Madame Lhoumeau was given the task of buying a triple-faced mirror, which she assured us every American woman possessed. At the last moment there were some heated discussions about the flowers that Mother and old Marie had used to decorate the guests' room, as I was of the opinion (and quite rightly so) that they had overdone and transformed the room into a Corpus Christi altar, a florist's greenhouse, or, worse still, into a funeral parlor. The priestesses compromised; the bouquets were kept, and the seven or eight vases of supplementary flowers that their solicitude had gathered together in Stefan and Nora's bedroom.

Yes, Nora was as beautiful as we had imagined her to be, as beautiful as the photo in the leather frame that Stefan had placed on the nighttable as he arranged his things in their room, all to the stupefaction of old Marie. "It isn't enough for him to have his lady with him, he has to have her in a photo on the other side of the bed!" In life as in the photo, she had long silken hair of a blond that is neither golden nor ripe straw, but more the color of lime-blossom at the end of blooming, or of a somewhat faded golden ochre of the kind that oak trees scatter about in autumn, like dancing tresses whose radiance, like Nora's, seemed to come from the inside.

Old Marie and her niece and Matthew took up the couple's baggage, going into ecstasies over the chocolate brown valises decorated with constellations of small gold stars, the bags of supple leather, and the appurtenances of luxury and unfamiliar refinements that had never made an appearance when Stefan came to Breuil by himself, with his usual baggage, the eternal two-suiter and the overly weighty suitcase filled with papers and books.

We had forgotten one detail, namely that Nora spoke only English and Spanish, and I had tried in vain to conquer the latter language and to retain the rudiments of English, but I always carried on conversations with Stefan in French. During Stefan and Nora's stay in Breuil, conversations took place through smiles, pidgin French, gestures, and renewed smiles. Nora's smile, with her eyes of pale periwinkle blue and the graciousness of her face when she leaned gently to one side as a sign of concentration when she did not comprehend, or her schoolgirl attention directed toward Stefan when he explained something to her in English or in Spanish, all put us under the spell of her charm, but it was a rather vague charm stemming from a communication that was too limited. I would have liked to ask Nora a thousand questions and to have listened to her talk ad infinitum. I sat there in silence, smiling at her or smiling at Stefan who spoke to me about Nora in Nora's presence, as he tried to play two roles, that of a Nora reduced to silence, and his own of a Stefan speaking for two.

Stefan did the honors at Breuil, showing Nora everything from the hayloft to the outbuildings, from the agricultural structures to the fields. The first evening of their visit, he wanted Nora to preside over the ritual ceremony of resetting the clock with the slender Doric columns in the large livingroom: after having wound the mechanism with the little black key, you advance the big hand with your finger, knowing full well that you will have to do it all over again the next day. Nora laughed at the explanations that Stefan made to her, and which we managed to figure out. Her lighthearted laughter would spiral like some strange singing butterfly that is clearly not a butterfly, but a bird, a wren.

Meals were friendly, comical, and tiring at the same time. Mother's questions to Nora, translated and explained by Stefan, came so clearly from another planet from the one the young woman had lived on, that they must have appeared to her kindly but preposterous, and without any real possibility of response. One thing that Mother asked Nora was where she had gotten the autumn-leaf dress that she wore for dinner, and when Nora gave her the name of a prominent Milanese couturier established in New York, Mother commented that couturiers like that had become almost non-existent in France, because no one wanted to sew any more, so that everyone had to purchase ready-made clothes. It was the same when Nora admired the garden, specifically the photos of it during summertime, because the Christmas roses are a legend, and asked the name of the gardener, Mother had a problem explaining that she had Matthew turn over the soil and do the fertilizing as he had the responsibility for heavy work, but that she herself was her own gardener.

We lived several days of charm, intimacy, and misunderstandings. But I was happy despite the false notes of the visit, despite the pale winter sun that denied us the White Christmas we had dreamed about, happy because Stefan and Nora were radiant with tender fire. It seemed my friend had been given a gift of something I had never dreamed of for myself, a love match shared with this long-bodied young woman who was so beautiful and so *luxurious* that she seemed almost out of place in a pleasant way—in our old gray house.

What struck all of us was the metamorphosis of Stefan. He had aged a bit, and at the same time he had become younger. He seemed charged through with a joyous electricity. Joy bubbled in him, and it had been a long time since I had heard such laughter at Breuil. Stefan and Nora's laughter resounded like intermingled caresses. Stefan made Mother and old Marie laugh, and the house rang with rejoicing.

Stefan came into my little office where the operating accounts and the agronomical books lay side by side with his books and my modest library. He said that Argentina was a highly *unlikely* country, a sorcerer's cauldron out of which could come either the best or the worst, but that on coming back from Germany, he had told himself that, all the same, it was not his fatherland, but it was his country, and that he would not look for any other. He was boiling over with ideas and projects. He was then writing his book *The Dead Angle of History*, the dead angle of what one does not see behind oneself, plus what one does not see in time-and-space, by one's very side, or ahead of oneself (and sometimes within oneself).

"What is as fascinating as the great visionaries or those gifted with second sight, and whose prophecies have been confirmed by the march of history," he said, "are the great *lapses* of men who in appearance are the most lucid and the best prepared to comprehend, but who are also often as blind as the rest of ignorant humanity. The French writer-politician Condorcet wrote in 1784, five years before the Revolution, that *'wars and revolutions will become less frequent in the future.'* That was an illusion. But what is quite obvious from a distance is often not apparent to the actors in the drama at the time. Christians pillaging Byzantium in 1204 thought they were serving Christianity. They were strengthening Islam. At the assembly of the Estates-General in 1614, people thought the door had been slammed on revolution in France as well as elsewhere. But preparations for the Thirty Years' War, the uprisings and peasant revolts in Russia, in addition to the civil wars of England and the Fronde in France were already under way. Everything will start up again, and it's not over. France thought in 1919 that her victory had gained her the first place in Europe. She did not recognize that the bloodbath of the First War had reduced her to a small or medium-sized nation. Writing a history of men's blindness might be the most efficacious of treatises on tolerance and prudence. . . .

"Or it would be better still," he went on, "to complete La

Boetie's *Treatise on Voluntary Servitude* by a *Treatise on Voluntary Blindness*. Humanity displays an admirable ingenuity in the invention of sham problems in order to avoid facing and resolving the real ones, in combating heresies rather than shortages and famines, in hunting witches rather than fighting the plague, in persecuting Jews rather than undoing traps in the economy.

"Of course," he concluded, "if I undertake to write the history of our species' blindnesses, there is one blindness that I will never overcome: my own."

I remember one evening at Breuil when Stefan was in a very good mood. He was miming The Thinker behind whose back an Evil Genie was doing dirty tricks, and who tries to turn around quickly enough to catch the malicious jokester in the act. He was playing the role of Plato extolling Socrates' freedom of spirit and praising justice. Plato senses that something is going on behind his back. He suddenly turns around and discerns the Tyrant Denys of Syracuse executing one of his critics under a banner proclaiming "Plato mit uns!" Equally fine was the role of Machiavelli, played by Stefan, when he discovered that the Prince he had created to defend the Republic was busily overthrowing it and replacing it with a dictatorship. He made a pretense of decking himself out with an imaginary square beard and mimicked Marx expounding on his theory of the withering away of the State, at the same time the State rises behind his back like a pyramid reaching so high that its summit, like the tower of Babel, gets lost in the clouds. Mother undoubtedly did not understand all the allusions of the charade, but laughed as wholeheartedly as Nora and I did.

Those long days of the Christmas holidays with their chilly winter and our Breuil ringing with laughter left me a kind of memory of a radiant end of autumn, a lengthy gaiety that was no longer expected. The stranger who initially had intimidated Breuil had brought to it a youthfulness that I thought was lost forever. The electricity that flowed between Stefan and Nora was something that all of us inhabiting the old house felt. Love makes lovable not only the beloved, not only the lovers.

A year later we learned about the birth of Sara. The child was ten years old when Nora became seriously ill. Cancer carried her off in six months. She was forty-eight. I had thought of trying to persuade Stefan to come to Europe to stay awhile at Breuil, but he turned down my invitation. "I would be hard to put up with I am so heavy-hearted." I guessed as well that he would find renewing the memory of that happy Christmas holiday unbearable today. As he came out of the daze of his despair, he threw himself into his work, and passionately devoted himself to the care of little Sara, whose pictures in the photographs he sent me had a startling resemblance to Nora.

Stefan's serious books are the best known ones, his essay on *The State of the Law,* his memoirs entitled *A Man between Two Worlds,* his major work on the genocides of history, *The Politics of the Tabula Rasa.* It was one of Stefan's students, Angel Tomás, whom I met through him in Paris, who talked to me about a less well known aspect of Stefan's

113

work. As a childhood friend of Stefan and Nora's daughter, Angel recalled that two years after his wife's death, Stefan created a marionette theater for Sara and her little friends every Sunday. Angel was still filled with wonder as he recalled the plays that Stefan had written: *The Girl Who Lived in a Thimble*, *The Forest of Clocks* and above all, *The Adventures of Mister Gray, the Cowboy Cat*. The latter had been conceived at first as a one-act play that would fill a single afternoon, but its success was so triumphant that Stefan had to prolong it for several weeks. But Stefan's dramatic work has left hardly any traces, except in Sara's remembrances of childhood and those of half a dozen other young people. One died under torture, three others have disappeared, and two more live in exile.

Stefan rarely returned to Europe during Sara's formative years. He made one quick trip to Oxford for the bestowal of a degree *honoris causa*. He phoned me from London, but he did not want to leave Sara alone too long and apologized for not making a hop down to Breuil. His letters became more frequent than in previous years, all of them full of the child, and of the problems he was having with education and pedagogy. He wanted her to know the same languages that he did, because, he said, the structuring of my life has given me at least that advantage that I would like to share with Sara, that of being able (as I hope) to communicate with several hundred million of my contemporaries (but does one always want to? he added). By the same token, Stefan was afraid of crushing Sara under too many demands and too much work. But she did not seem to suffer from too much studying or from the private lessons that he had given to her, and he was delighted that by her fifteenth year she could speak not only Spanish and German, but English almost to perfection, and reasonably good French as well.

Sara was eighteen years old in 1975. Stefan wanted her to begin her studies at Harvard, and then for her to have a long stay in France. He was upset by her opposition to his projects, but explained to me only vaguely in his letters what made the girl want to stay in Buenos Aires. "She has friends here whom she doesn't want to leave," he said. I assumed that she was in love. She may have been, but that was not what her father was talking about, as I was to learn later on. Nevertheless, toward the end of 1975, Sara seemed to have made up her mind to enroll at Harvard. Stefan wrote me that he was going to make a "sentimental journey" to the United States with his daughter. But in September, he unexpectedly landed in Paris, accompanied by Sara. He had had warning signs of cardiac problems on his return to Buenos Aires, Sara told me on the phone, and Doctor Boroa had wanted, no, not wanted, *ordered* him to go to Paris to consult a specialist named Pranté, and the latter had immediately put Stefan in the Pitié Hospital under his care. "Is it serious?" Sara hoped not, but was sure of nothing. I took the train for Paris.

Stefan seemed worn out. His face was lined, his breath short, and his skin slightly bilious as he lay in his hospital bed, but Doctor Pranté reassured me. He told me that he had hospitalized Stefan to facilitate the examinations that he wanted to undertake as completely and rapidly as possible, and that it was easier to handle things there. I stayed in Paris for several days, and went to see Stefan every day.

Rest helped him to regain strength, plus good care. I met Sara. She looked more and more like Nora.

Once the examinations were completed, Pranté prescribed treatment, a diet for tension and, above all—something practically essential, he said—a major and lengthy rest, cutting himself off from everything as much as possible. "You must relax." "Doctor, you remind me of specialists in beauty treatments who recommend that their clients avoid annoyances, worries, grief, and stress, all of which cause wrinkles and a bad complexion. It is not I who created the tensions, it's the world I live in. . . ." "I agree," said Doctor Pranté, "but if you want to continue to live in the world and to go on with the struggle, you must come to a stop for a while. Otherwise . . ."

I encouraged Stefan to follow Pranté's advice, which was the same as that of Boroa, whom Stefan had phoned: "Stay in France six months or a year. María Teresa (Stefan's executive secretary) can take good care of the office, and you have an excellent staff working for you. You are overworked. Take a little care of yourself. . . ."

I invited Stefan to come stay at Breuil, but I sensed that he had a problem to be solved. He had long conversations with Sara in the hotel where he had gone after leaving the hospital.

"My father," she confided in me, "can't bring himself to ask me, but I sense that what he wants, if he stays on in Paris, is for me to reverse my program of studies and to enroll at the Sorbonne instead of Harvard. If I accept, I'll have the feeling I've let down my friends." Then she added, as though for me what was clarity itself, "I'm active in the

'OO,' you know? But if I refuse, I'll have the feeling I've let down my father."

I had to get back to Breuil. Mother had the flu. Stefan phoned me that Sara had decided to stay in Paris. He had found a small furnished apartment in the Rue Guynemer, near the Luxemburg Gardens, for them both. Sara made a short trip to Buenos Aires to gather up her and her father's personal belongings. When I went to Paris for the annual Exposition of Farm Equipment, I found them settled in. Stefan still had hollowed lines and breathed with difficulty. As I was leaving the apartment, I ran into Doctor Pranté at the door: "He can regain his strength rapidly," he said. "He has resources. Above all he needs quiet, rest, and having his daughter with him."

At the end of March 1976, a new military coup in Buenos Aires was announced. I called Stefan right away. "This time could be worse than the others. Knowing the generals of this junta, I can tell you it's the extreme right of the army that has taken over."

Stefan's voice was deep and hoarse, and his breathing labored. Events in Argentina were not going to help Stefan get well. Coups d'état cause heart attacks.

"There is one thing that makes me very happy," he said. "It's having Sara here. They didn't hold her hostage."

·8·

I had to admit to myself that it was not only Stefan's being in Paris, but his illness that had brought him closer to me again. Naturally he received visits from people much more important than I—politicians, writers, and editors. But when I went to Paris, and I did frequently that year under various pretexts, the moments I spent with him gave me a happiness that made me feel ashamed. The weakness of those we love gives us a hold over them. I tried not to tire Stefan, and so stayed with him for short periods each visit. But my friend was my friend as he had not been for a long time.

It's true that he had a hard winter. It rained a great deal that year, and Paris was humid under its cloudy skies. Stefan found it hard to breathe. "What is tiresome about a feeling of suffocation, in organic *distress*," he said, "is that the spirit always suggests good reasons to the body for being distressed. By the same token, when health is good and you can breathe fully, the spirit furnishes the body with excellent motives for being happy." Stefan had few of those motives for happiness, except Sara's presence. Pranté made

119

frequent calls on Stefan. He insisted that his patient con-
serve his energies, and that he stay in bed or stretched out
most of the day. "My carcass may be resting, Doctor, but my
mind is in constant motion, and I can't get it to *rest.*" Every
day, or almost every day, Stefan was in contact with his
office. I would go into the adjoining room while he called
Buenos Aires or received a call from over there. I began to
feel that I knew that María Teresa at the other end of the
line. Stefan discussed business affairs, dossiers, and defense
strategies. "They're hopeless battles," he said. "Lodge a
complaint? Against whom? Most of the time, we don't
know who did the arresting, who imprisons, where, or why.
Start court proceedings? There are no tribunals, no courts,
no trials. You have to act as though the situation were
normal, hang up the phone, jot down the date, and badger
those people in power that can be reached. My 'children,'
los hijos (as he called his collaborators, mostly young people
who had been students of his), are tenacious and coura-
geous, but they are defenseless. . . ." He said to Pranté,
"Come on, Doctor, let me go join 'my unit.' I have the
feeling that I'm deserting them by staying here." "You
would be more of a hindrance to them than a help. I'll let
you go once you have recovered, but you're going to have to
be patient. I'm not going to ship your colleagues a sick man
to care for. They have enough to worry about as it is."

After he had hung up the phone and left María Teresa as
though she were just in an adjoining room, Stefan would
say that talking with her gave him the impression of smell-
ing the odor of a waiting room, what he called an odor of
impending calamity. "It's particularly strong in the office on

Saturdays," he said, "because it's market day, but most of the lawyers have left town for the weekend as of Friday night. By the end of Saturday afternoon, our waiting room smells of sheep fat, moist raw wool, perspiration, pepper, unguents of mountain herbs, cold tobacco, and *maté* tea.

"There is always," he added, "the current of small matters to be brought to court, but without much chance of winning the case. Justice in Argentina does not like the odor of adversity. The poor smell too strongly. The lawyers who defend the poor, like the doctors who care for them, make serious people shrug their shoulders." Stefan's colleagues continued to see workers fired from their jobs without having been paid, tenants thrown out into the street, and *poenes* cornered by loansharks. But every month the number of *desaparecidos* increased, leaving the wife of a union member whose husband had disappeared from the face of the earth, the widow of a teacher whose mutilated body was found in a suburb, the family of an agronomist carried off by some unknown persons who came to "arrest" him one night and who was never seen again. How to plead a case and where, for the disappeared who had had no opportunity to present themselves before a tribunal, and who are in the hands of inaccessible people?

One evening when we were about to have dinner, Stefan said to me "Stay here" when the telephone rang. It was María Teresa calling from Buenos Aires. He handed me the receiver a moment. "It's five-thirty in the afternoon there." In the distance we could hear a concert of horn-honking. He took back the phone and spoke with María Teresa. When he finished the conversation, he said: "Do you suppose that happy sound of horns was a manifestation of protest? No, it was simply the parade of cars of team supporters in Florida Street following the limousines bringing back the national soccer team from Ezeiza Airport and celebrating their victory in the match for the International Cup. Soccer for everybody, something to eat, winning the lottery for the poor, going to the beach for the rich, that's what's on the nation's mind." Stefan was only too right. For the most part, the kidnappings, the murders, all that was passed over or took second place. Alonso's tendon or the team's right-center was of much greater concern to the public than the discovery of a mutilated body disfigured by a machete. The great "political" news was the announcement that the Soviet team Dynamo would be coming soon to confront the top Argentinian team. The army and the political police are the pillars of the state. Soccer and the lottery are the two pillars of society. Circus games for all, bread for a few, and torture for malcontents. . . .

Sara spent time with her father toward the end of the afternoon even if she were going out later on. She had made contact with comrades from Argentina, and through them formed friendships with young French people who belonged to leftist groups similar to the one she had been active in at home. Father and daughter loved each other tenderly, and the proof of it was in their almost perpetual confrontations, which went from bantering to passionate political debate in which the adversaries made concessions proportionately less as they loved proportionately more, and both had enough resources of affection to have no need to hold back in the discussion.

Sara usually was disguised as a *clocharde de luxe*, with faded jeans painstakingly torn to tatters and artfully cut short with scissors, a man's shirt too long for her worn outside the jeans, sneakers, and with an elastic band around her ponytail. And in that American-style charade of sham poverty for a poor little rich girl appeared the face of Nora, and her way of knitting her brows when she was puzzled or of radiating sunshine when she rejoiced in something. Sara was Nora at the same age. Nora had been barely two years older than Sara when Stefan had met her. Sara squinted when she wanted to concentrate, exactly like Nora. She already had the beginnings of those little crow's feet at the corners of her eyes that had caused me to think when I had first met her mother: "A person with those little lines is someone who has already smiled a lot in her lifetime, even when life didn't smile at her." I pondered over what I knew of Nora's childhood which had been torn apart by divorced parents who fought over her. At the age of eleven, she had left her father's house, taken the train all by herself, crossed half of the United States, and taken refuge in her grandparents' home in Vermont. She had informed her father and her mother by letter that from then on she would welcome their visits on alternate dates that she would decide herself. The judge who had heard the grandparents' lawyer read the little girl's letter had decided purely and simply to confirm the terms dictated by the child. "There are moments," said Stefan, "when I am tempted to confirm purely and simply the judgment that Sara has made of society, even if I find the means she chooses to carry out those judgments absurd and harmful.

"All the same," he added, "Jewish blood mixed with Irish blood can give impressive results!"

In a discussion with Sara, Stefan gave an ironic and slightly bitter description of the situation before the last coup d'état.

"The Communist Party was piously reciting the prayers of their Marxist-Leninist rosary and providing the government with a critical support that was neither supportive nor critical, while they lethargically maneuvered an attempt to form a coalition government composed of 'true democrats' and of 'patriotic' and 'progressive' military men."

"Papa," said Sara, "who still believes in the communists? They abandoned the revolution a long time ago."

"The revolution that you think you embody! The *Organización Obrera,* just as its name indicates, disrupts the work of some hundred workers, trotted out for pampering like rare specimens by a thousand students and young people of the bourgeoisie."

"My father," said Sara with an aggressiveness tempered by a smile, "my father contradicts himself constantly. He makes fun of the socialist countries where class origin is an indelible flaw, where there is a racism of genealogy, and he reproaches the Workers Organization for also recruiting the middle class. But it's the turncoats from the middle class who furnish the extra help that make the victory of the masses possible in every revolution."

Stefan took me as witness.

"You understand, Etienne, that Sara and all her *companions* have the expressions 'masses,' 'mass action,' 'pressure by the masses,' 'organization of the masses' on their lips all the time. But the masses are crushed in misery and divided between peasants and city dwellers, and people from the South and people from the North. The masses are afraid of civil war. They know that between the repressions of the right and the guerrilla warfare of the left they, as always, will be caught in the pincers. Before the putsch, the country was paralyzed and tetanized. Everybody saw the danger advancing, without seeing any solution other than submission on the one hand or death for heroes and madmen (often one and the same) on the other."

"It may just be stereotyped language, but when the terms 'masses,' 'people,' 'poor,' are used, they always signify the same thing: the millions who have no right to express themselves."

"In whose name do you speak—you, the Trotskyites, the unionists, the Peronists of the left, the Peronists of the right, the progressive Catholics, and the who-knows-what-else, in a cacophony accompanied by a concert of machine guns?"

"Are you reproaching our activists for their courage?"

"No. For their confusion of spirit and their total lack of strategy."

"The oo has a clearly defined strategy."

"What tendency, what current, what nuance of the oo?" asked Stefan with an affectionate irony. "The politico-military branch that leans toward Mao? The Jorge Farmiento group meeting on the platform of the Second Congress of the left-wing faction of the National Delegation of the Fourth Congress? Or the secessionists of the *Nueva Organización Obrera* under the leadership of Felipe O'Neill, already excluded from the NOO after the last intervention of Taco the Shark in the last governing committee meeting?"

"Do you think you're being funny, Papa? Reread Marx's life, and you'll see that the history of the First International is a series of scissions, divisions, and factional struggles. Revolutionary movements are born in contradiction."

"They are born in a bureaucracy, in a ruling class that's more narrow-minded than the previous one, they're born in terror and poverty, an equal and egalitarian poverty, poverty of men, of ideas, of consumer goods, poverty of elementary liberties and of breathable air."

"You keep playing the same old record," said Sara with rage. "It's precisely because our experience and our analyses have shown us the cause of these errors that we are sufficiently well armed now to avoid the return to such things. We ponder a great deal on all aspects of the Organization studying what *our* socialism will be like."

"But while you're waiting, the OO thinks of the masses, and decides more quickly than the masses, while it shoots in the name of the masses more quickly than the police. Your activists have had more heart than brain. They get themselves killed very bravely. For the future. If by accident that future were to come into being and were to resemble your project, I'd have cold chills."

Sara knits her brows like Nora. She has her mother's eyes when, said Stefan, they "flashed knives of blue steel."

"And the growth of Fascism on our continent doesn't give you cold chills?" said the girl with vehemence. "In your youth you have Hindenburg bringing Hitler to power. In front of you you have big money bringing back the Fascist generals into power, and what obsesses you is a stage in the development of the workers' movement and the liberation movements that have been gone through some time ago!"

"May you speak the truth!" whispered Stefan.

I sensed that even in Sara's absence Stefan was debating with her. "You know Pascal's phrase," he said: " 'I believe only those witnesses who get their own throats cut.' But heroism is not a guarantee of veracity, nor is courage necessarily linked to intelligence. And witnesses who get their own throats cut usually have a tendency to become cutthroats themselves, if they feel that they can justify it as a political and historical necessity. For years now there has been a great turbulence in Argentina due to cutters of throats and those with their throats cut, the guerrilla fighters and Trotskyites, the armed groups of union members whether of the left, the center, or the right, the Catholic terrorists of the right fighting the partisans of the Second Vatican Council, the armed groups of defense for the Catholics of the left, the death squads. The killers are shot down, the half-hearted are liquidated, the softies are executed, those who condemn violence are slaughtered, the Fascists are machine-gunned, liberal politicians who call for calm are killed, and leftist journalists who have protested the murder of liberal politicians are pumped full of bullets. It never stops. The Triple A, the so-called Argentinian Anticommunist Alliance, kills the guerrilla fighters, slaughters their lawyers, executes legalistic politicians, and machine-guns newspapermen who protest. Naturally, in this game, it's those who have the most efficient arms and ammunition, and the fewest complicated ideas who win—

that is, the army. Our military men have excellent American equipment and an ideology that has been proven. Any critical soul is a *subversive*, all subversives should be wiped out, everyone on the left, every liberal, is an ally of the communists, and all Jews are accomplices of the left and the liberals. The presiding general of the Junta has declared that Argentina has three principal enemies: Karl Marx, because he tried to destroy Christian society, Freud because he tried to destroy the Christian family, and Einstein because he tried to destroy the Christian concept of space and time."

"Do you think you can reason with imbeciles like that or persuade such fanatics?" asked Sara. "Only arms can make them surrender."

"On condition that you have more arms and more powerful ones than they do."

"Liberals always begin by preaching prudence and the reasoned calculation of the strength of the opposition, and end up making compromises."

"I know," said Stefan, "that the path between two biological stages is a narrow one: between youth that has the talent for anger and the weakness of impatience, and old age that sometimes has the talent for lucidity and often has the weakness of resignation."

Stefan was suddenly worn out from the discussion, and Sara reproached herself for getting overheated. She tenderly kissed her father and went back to work in her room.

Stefan had begun taking notes for a book when he arrived in Paris, and had, I believe, already written a few pages. But when I asked him about what he was writing, he admitted that he had stopped work on it. "I'm waiting until I get well to allow myself to think on serious matters. I am too much afraid that the fits and starts of my machinery will be reflected in my work, and that the image I have of the world and the one I would present will be distorted by the irregularities of that capricious little muscle, the heart. If I express historical pessimism, I would prefer that it not be because of this unreasonable carcass of mine."

From time to time he would talk again about going back to work. On other occasions he would tell Doctor Pranté that he ought to go back to Buenos Aires. "You are free, dear friend, but I would not advise it . . ." the doctor would answer. One morning he found Stefan preparing his clothes and belongings. He was standing by his bed, breathless, his face wrinkled, and his eyes rimmed with red. His smile was weary: "I was trying to pack my bags to go back to Argentina, but I no sooner started than I wore myself out."

He began avoiding serious discussions with Sara and her friends. "It's due to fatigue," he told me, "but it's also because I'm afraid of contaminating others. The reality is somber enough. I'm afraid that the sorry state of my health will make it blacker still. Illness distorts judgment and maligns life. Does health distort one's view by overly beautifying things?"

Nevertheless, I had to return to Breuil. Matthew and Maurice were taking care of the farming. Old Marie more or less took care of the house. But there was still the administration of the property to see to, tax reports to be filled out and purchases to be made. I went about my

129

paperwork without enthusiasm, but my mind was only on getting back to Paris.

Stefan seemed to have given us the activities of the office in Buenos Aires. The news from there, however, grew bleaker and bleaker. The *chupados*, the people who had been *swallowed up*, could now be counted in the thousands. The terror cast a pall like a heavy layer of noxious gas over daily life. "But from here," he said, "I don't have a clear enough view of things to interfere in the decisions of my colleagues."

Troubles with balance had further complicated Stefan's cardiac problems. He would begin to feel dizzy without any warning and would have to sit down right away, suddenly extremely pale. "It's like a storm lantern that pitches about in a tempest. Could it be that that is what death is, the abrupt snuffing out of the lantern?"

Pranté had Stefan put back in the hospital and put him through a series of examinations. "What I am afraid of," he confided to me, "is that the treatment necessary for the problems of balance is counter-indicated by the heart treatments."

The doctors did, however, find a proper treatment, and by spring Stefan seemed to be better. I proposed to the doctor that we take him to Breuil. He did not oppose the trip. Stefan was still quite weak, but he had begun to put on a little weight. Every day he took a walk with me, and he was sleeping regularly if insufficiently after months when his breathing had kept him up a part of the night. Marie took him his breakfast in bed every morning. Her simple concept of health was to eat well to keep up one's energy, and she tried to *nourish* Monsieur Stefan. She would set a little plate with toast spread with potted meat rillettes, made when "the pig was killed," on the tray with his tea (that drink that she had never so much as tasted, she said proudly, except when she had had pneumonia in 1926). Stefan would pretend to nibble a bit to satisfy Marie, but he really had no appetite.

I would look at him lying there, pale and fragile, propped up against the pillows and covered by the red down comforter, and I could not keep myself—seeing the slow pace of his movements, his way of closing his eyes without sleeping, and the breathing that was a bit too heavy—from thinking of Mother before her final crisis when a great feeling of weakness would surge up inside her. When he finished his breakfast, pushing away the tray on which what he had not touched—almost everything—remained, I would tiptoe out of the room. But sometimes I would hear him whisper, without opening his eyes: "Stay a while longer if you have nothing pressing. . . ." Alas, I never had anything more pressing.

"You see," he said to me on one of the mornings that I had stayed with him, "it's not the leave-taking that distresses me sometimes. It's having to leave with the feeling that everything that I have done since I left Germany has been in vain. Everything that I've done, everything that I have tried to do, to explain, to render comprehensible. I say to myself that if I have such a destructive impression of discouragement and despair, it's because my body is discouraged, because my lungs are in despair at never filling with fresh air any more, and because my heart is like an old

131

motor that coughs, and because I think that the world has no more value than the image given by binoculars with dirty and mist-covered lenses."

"You know very well that this is just a moment to go through. The doctor is confident that you are going to be better soon. The proof is he gave permission for you to leave him, and Paris, and the hospital. . . ."

"Yes, yes," said Stefan (that *yes* that does not mean *yes*, but remains hanging in the air, questioning and evasive), and he continued his thought in a low voice:

"When I discovered years ago in Nietzsche's 'The Eternal Return of the Same,' *Ewige Wiedergeburt des Gleichen*, what astonished me was the kind of happiness, of surprising jubilation that Nietzsche felt at the idea, that love for a destiny he based on eternal recurrence. I worked arduously to disprove that insane theory, and to demolish the false proofs that Nietzsche thought he had found in astronomy, physics, and biology. I wanted to replace it with a concept of entropy that would make the idea of Eternal Recurrence absurd. But I have lived more than half a century now, crossed the ocean, set foot on soil so different from Old Europe's terrain—and everything that I thought I had fled from and hoped had been condemned forevermore is beginning all over again."

I objected, "That's because it's a country that is backward and has a very short history. It doesn't prove a thing. You always said and wrote yourself that nations are not all contemporary at one and the same time, that such-and-such a kingdom in Africa is in our sixth century, while

Finland is already in the twenty-first century, and that there is no *simultaneity* of progress. . . ."

"A miserable country, yes," said Stefan. "It was founded on extermination, and what is left of the Indians is a handful of tribes that have been reduced to penury and who are forced to lead the life of beasts of burden and of two-cent subjects for tourists' cameras. The history of the Great Nation is a web of petty atrocities, of score settlings disguised as battles, of fights between cowherds cutting one another open with knives and that are presented like the duel between Achilles and Agamemnon with all sorts of overblown blustering. Everything is a mess, the sewage system, the plumbing, the surfacing of the streets, the conscience of those who do the governing, and the spine of those who are governed. Everything can be bought with a 'bite,' *mordida,* from the Presidency of the Republic to a driver's license. Outside of Buenos Aires, the towns are ugly and dirty, the countryside is verminous and dusty, the faces of the middle class ooze with sluggish rapaciousness and those of the poor with a fatigue mixed with humiliation. It isn't a country yet; it's still vague terrain! But it isn't what that country has about it that is archaic and savage behind its modern facade that overwhelms you: it is precisely what is modern about it and contemporary. Barbarians come to grips with barbarity. But what happened with Hitler and what is happening in that unfortunate country right now is an ultramodern and wholly radical form of barbarity. The principle of the Final Solution of the Nazis was *Night and Mist.* They wanted what they condemned to disappear

133

forever, to become invisible, to have no place or even ever to have existed."

"And all the same, they did not succeed. The existence of the camps became public knowledge. . . ."

"For how long? Here and there you hear people denying their existence. . . . In Argentina the principle in action is *disappearance*. The 'subversives,' the Reds, the psychiatrists, the liberals, the Jews automatically suspected of being liberal, Reds, psychiatrists or Zionists, *disappear*, in the literal sense. One of our generals expressed it clearly: 'In this type of anti-subversive struggle, a cloud of silence should cloak everything.' What is taking place all over again in Argentina, 'The Eternal Return of the Same,' is what we supposed had been uprooted and forever condemned in 1945. History repeats itself like a broken record. . . ."

Stefan had kept his eyes closed while he was talking. When he opened them again, he tried to smile at me.

"Pardon me for musing out loud," he said. "It's fatigue."

"Rest a while," I said, and quietly left the room.

By the end of spring, Stefan was decidedly better. I went with him to Paris where he settled back into the Rue Guynemer. Sara had been interested in a summer course at the University of California at Berkeley, but changed her mind about going so as not to leave her father alone. He, on the contrary, encouraged her to go to America, assuring her that nothing could help him more to get well than feeling that he was leaving Sara free. The latter had found a Spanish "governess" named Blanca who had quickly and efficiently taken over the running of the household and had adopted Stefan like an elderly child whom one both re-

134

spects and spoils. Stefan had decided to take up work on his book again, and to spend the summer in Paris ("the best season of all," he said, "Paris delivered from her ever-present Parisians)," so he could work in the National Library. Pranté did not intend to take his vacation until September and would pay Stefan a call every day.

Stefan had recovered his energy, even his customary gaiety, in spite of the long-armed, heavy shadow of what was going on in Buenos Aires. If he had not regained hope, at least he had recovered that courtesy of uncertain hope that hides its uncertainty to keep it from becoming contagious. He seemed to me to be so much back in step that I resolved not to change my bachelor habits, and made the decision to go, as I had every year, to take my three-week cure at the spa in La Bourboule.

I phoned from the hotel every two or three days to talk with Stefan, who was working, profitably, he said. He felt so good, he told me, that he was going to London for a few days to consult some documents he needed in the British Museum. He would call me when he got back.

·9·

Stefan had gone to such pains to keep from Sara, from his friends, and from his doctor his decision to return to Argentina after he learned of María Teresa's disappearance and that the government was sitting pretty pretending to know nothing about the matter. When Stefan's friends showed proof that he had indeed taken the Paris–Buenos Aires flight and that he had not been seen again since the plane's arrival, a government spokesman answered that Professor Stein had landed at Buenos Aires in transit and had taken off that same day for an unknown destination.

The presidency's spokesman ironically commented on the "squawking of the pseudo-democrats," the supporters of a corrupt regime that had plunged the country into economic and social chaos and made necessary the intervention of the government in a "National Reconstruction." He railed against the hypocritical snivellers who invent imaginary victims but forget to have pity for the crucified body of a nation that for many years had been the prey of subversion and treason. That particular spokesman was an obscure journalist who had had his writings rejected everywhere year after year. Now he dictated his communiqués to the press with the pride of an author who has finally received his just recognition, in the photos haughtily holding high his bald yellowing skull with its three surviving wisps of hair plastered down.

When he was questioned on the whereabouts of Professor Stein, he categorically denied that the latter had been arrested, much less executed. In a voice that was meant to be ingratiating but was anything but to the reporters and foreign correspondents present, he suggested that Professor Stein was possibly enjoying a romantic adventure. Actually, the spokesman insinuated, we have known for some years about the presence of a young very elegant woman at Stein's side.

"His secretary, Mariá Teresa Alvarez," remarked the correspondent from the *Washington Post,* "is under arrest at the present time in Good Shepherd Prison."

"You seem to be better informed than I am," said the spokesman with a note of bitterness in his voice.

"If you are badly informed, then don't give us any funny business," said the American insolently.

The spokesman had his orders: to get along with the Americans. "Even if they pull a few things, they definitely gave us a green light," the President had said, "and we're going to need them." Consequently, the spokesman changed the subject.

In the days that followed, government officials had trouble orchestrating their responses concerning Stefan's fate.

As an answer to a question posed by a journalist from the

United Press, the head of the press office made a statement that left everybody incredulous: Stefan Stein must have committed suicide. For some time he had been subject to periods of depression, the general had confided. Stein knew that the Security Forces had very compromising documents about his connections with foreign powers. He must have ended his days before the proofs of his complicity could be made public.

The American reporter had asked if the government was going to publish those documents. The spokesman had answered that it was up to the Commission for Inquiry into Antinational Activities to make that decision. Personally the President was in favor of an amnesty in view of the services that Stefan Stein had previously rendered to the country. Yes, the general was an advocate of avoiding further references to the weaknesses that might not prove an act of treason by the Professor, but which, all the same, would show how, like many other naive intellectuals, Stein had allowed himself to be manipulated by the enemies of the National Spirit. The spokesman went on to point out that Professor Stein's sense of responsibility had undoubtedly been affected by the fact that he was of foreign birth. In spite of the naturalization that he had attained at an early age, he had never fully succeeded in truly assimilating the Essence of the Fatherland.

The Head of State's leniency astonished his interlocutors. His penetration and the delicacy of his psychology left them flabbergasted.

On the same day, the new Argentinian ambassador to Paris declared to a reporter tht Professor Stein might have been the victim of a settling of scores between rival groups of subversives. Most of the disappearances and the killings that had come to light were the result, the diplomat added, of tensions existing between irresponsible groups that were as dedicated to destroying one another as they were to undermining the foundations of the newly recovered national unanimity. Professor Stein had long been an unwitting toy in the hands of the communist sedition and the bolshevized unions. But the leftist factions and terrorists of the *Organización Obrera* had publicly accused Stein in their press of being an accomplice of *"reactionary conciliators."* In support of this hypothesis of the "execution" of Stein by a revolutionary brigade, the ambassador had taken out a dossier containing a clipping from a clandestine bulletin of a minor faction that spoke of the *"conscious treachery of the bourgeois democrat Stefan Stein."* The Junta's representative in Paris had concluded saying: "So you see, if crime there was, it bears a signature!"

When Sara learned of her father's disappearance, she left immediately for Buenos Aires. She besieged ministries, the bishopric, the newspapers, all without the least clarification. No one dared touch the daughter of the missing person, despite the pernicious uproar that she persisted in making.

Stefan Stein was never seen again.

· 10 ·

The conclusions of the National Commission named after the generals' fall from power to investigate their crimes and presided over by Ernesto Sabato made it possible to figure out what had happened in Stefan's case. It was through the reading of *Nunca Más*, the white book published by the Commission, that I learned much later what had gone on. And in those places where the *Comisión sobre la desaparición de personas* could not provide details or was limited to asking questions, the investigation undertaken on their own by Stefan's colleagues, which they shared with me, clarifies some of the shadowy areas of the tragedy.

It is evident that the overlapping of official or underground organizations complicated the investigators' job. After the generals' takeover, the Security Forces were unified in principle, but in reality, the three Security Forces continued to arrest, torture, and execute each on their own. One story goes that the men of the Military Security of the Infantry appeared at the door of an apartment at the same time as those of the Navy, and so the two groups

141

tossed a coin to see which one would arrest the "suspect."
As the Navy won, the victim was imprisoned, tortured, and
shot down in the cellars of the maritime arsenal instead of
the Headquarters of the Ground Forces.

In addition to the military police, the two services of
"civil" police, the procurers charged with judiciary proceedings, and the "legals" who had action brought against them
by the regime for National Order, there were also separate
networks comprised of a band of stoolpigeons—men for
hire and killers employed by the different services—plus the
Bureau of Information that was supposed to bring information together and keep files on the denunciations, whether
anonymous or signed, and the organization of the *Grupos de
Tareas* or Work Groups (no one spelled out what the word
"work" meant exactly. . .).

The investigations of the Commission gave proof that
the *Grupos de Tareas* had been directed by officers who
sometimes wore the uniform of the different Securities, but
who generally wore "civilian" clothes (if any word with
"civil" in it can be used in connection with their "work").
Civilian auxiliaries were recruited among the splinter
groups of the extreme right, and from among the beggars
and ex-convicts of the capital, who were promised pardons
for their offenses on condition that they participate in the
crimes of the *GT*, as the initiates called it.

Despite the horrors of the acts ascribed to the killers and
executioners set free during the black years, neither the
Commission nor later on the examining magistrate and the
courts of justice had any difficulty in pushing ahead their
investigations. Most of the persons interrogated, once the

first evidence became overwhelming, proved to be very talkative. They cooperated with their interrogators, "giving," without too much pressure, the names of their collaborators and accomplices in the hope, perhaps, of saving their own skins. That is how the denunciations of Major Cantón, one of the most sinister executioners of the Third Section of the Air Force, brought about the arrest of two personages who had succeeded for more than a year and a half in passing through the police traps. In photos published by the newspapers, Juan Aranda, called El Coyote, is a man heavy enough to be considered obese, some forty years old, with a forehead lacking lucidity and shortened by a bizarre little fringe of matted hair, small eyes (nervous, to judge by the photograph), all carved into a peaceably porcine face. According to their declarations, Camillo Gomez, nicknamed El Chico, a little fellow so deathly pale that you would have thought he was covered with flour, and much younger than El Coyote, was the whipping boy and assistant of the latter. He obeyed him in the "work" of the Dispensers of Justice as he had obeyed him in the diverse traffickings that had been carried out for years by the two men: handling stolen goods, procuring and the prostitution of minors of both sexes, then (more recently) drugs. It was after arresting El Coyote, who was caught trying to sell heroine by a policeman to whom he had forgotten to give the *mordida* tacitly agreed on to assure his silence, that Major Cantón had taken the latter into the *Grupos de Tareas*: El Coyote had had El Chico taken in with him, and the two men had participated at first in clandestine executions of the Dispensers of Justice and later on in the kidnap-

143

ping and "interrogations" thanks to which the dictatorship maintained its terror—and its pressure.

It was an inconceivable and naive blunder by the younger of the killers that brought about the discovery of their role in the matter of Stefan Stein. A photograph of Nora Stein was found thumbtacked to the wall of El Chico's room. It had been thrown into the dossier of the investigation of the affair along with other exhibits. Nora was recognized by one of the friends of the couple, Doctor Boroa, a member of the Commission. He himself interrogated El Chico.

"What was that photograph doing in your place?"

"It's a film star. I thought she was pretty."

"Where did you get that photo?"

"I don't remember any more. At the newspaper stand on the Paseo, I think. He sells postcards and photos of actors."

"Why are you lying? You know very well where this photo came from!"

The man was upset when the name of Stefan Stein was pronounced. He started to tremble, to stutter, and began to shake nervously all over.

"I had nothing to do with that stuff."

"What stuff! What are you referring to?"

"To nothing. I had nothing to do with any of that."

The little fellow was sent out, and El Coyote brought in. Boroa attacked him like a whiplash.

"Who gave you orders to *take care of* Professor Stein?"

El Coyote was visibly nonplussed by the abruptness of the question. But the form of the question gave the impression that there was, if not a way out, at least the possibility of

144

softening the blow.

He pretended to be trying to recall.

"Stefan Stein? . . . Stefan Stein?. . ."

He found it.

"Oh yes. I remember that Major Cantón said one day: 'There's a man named Stefan Stein who's supposed to land at the airport tomorrow. He's a German Jew who smeared our country's reputation in Europe. We have accounts to settle with him. But gently. Above all, not a hand on him. No beating up.'"

"And you took care of the matter 'gently'?"

"Me? I didn't do anything, don't even know Stein. All I know is that he was a Jew, and the major said he had spat on the flag. More than that, I don't know a thing about him."

It was at day's end, after two hours of interrogation and counter-interrogation going back and forth with the two men that Boroa and the members of the Commission got to the truth.

As the foot of the steps from the plane, an agent from Security dressed in civilian clothes had gone up to Stefan: "Sir, your friends are expecting you."

"But I didn't inform anyone," said Stefan, surprised.

"You were on the passenger list, and we thought we would spare you the formalities. If you would please get into my car. . ."

In the interrogation camp where Stefan was directly driven, the Chapel of the Virgin of Sorrows is between the antechamber for beatings and the room for "Special Operations for Maximum Interrogation," which is to say, torture. But Major Cantón had given orders: Professor Stein was to be treated without leniency, but also without brutality. Above all, they had to find out what contacts he expected to make on his arrival.

Stefan was conducted into an office where he found himself face to face with a heavy-set man with a forehead lined with a little fringe of shining hair, and a little deathly pale fellow with hair on end. "Laurel and Hardy," he must have thought.

"He wasn't touched. I swear to it!" said El Coyote. "He looked at us, turned pale, had an attack, and fell on the floor."

"I tried to revive him, but he was dead," said El Chico. "It must have been fear. I swear we didn't touch him. I swear it."

(After all, it may have been the truth . . .)

"And you went to tell the major?"

"We had to . . . What a time he gave us! Seems the general had given orders not to hurt Stefan Stein because that would have a bad effect outside the country. The major was furious. He told us: 'Take care of it yourself. I don't want to know about it. But Stein's never to be mentioned again.'"

"What did you do to get rid of the corpse?"

"It wasn't easy. But we had a buddy over at the Detention Center at Ezeiza on Ricchieri Avenue. He helped us."

"To do what?"

"We sprinkled the corpse with diesel oil and set fire to it."[1]

---

[1] Cf. *Nunca Más*, page 236, the deposition of the police agent Juan Carlos Urquiza. [Author's note.]

146

· 11 ·

Marie is slower and slower and deaf. And me, I'm more and more a stay-at-home and silent. I make a good couple with her. Her niece got married and left us. I pretend to give orders to Maurice and to Matthew. They know very well that they're the ones who keep the place going. When we had to replace the old tractor so we could keep the melons out of the vine stock, Maurice ordered the new tractor. He told me when it had been arranged: I had to go sign the papers with the salesman.

"Now you're being reasonable, Monsieur Etienne," said old Marie when she brought me my tea in the library. "You *chase around* less." What she calls *chasing* was going to Paris to see Stefan as I had been doing. The word *chasing* makes me smile, as if Marie suspected me of being a *skirt chaser*.

I hardly think at all. I mutter to myself over a few scant thoughts. I should not have left Stefan alone in Paris. . . . I ought to have guessed that he was getting ready to leave. . . . I ought to have understood sooner. . . .

147

Who says that hell does not exist? It opens up beneath our feet every time that we think, "I ought to have . . ."

I tried to talk about it to my brother when he came to sign the papers at the lawyer's for the sale of a piece of land at Les Coteaux that I was resigned to giving up. For once he listened to me. He concluded, "My poor Etienne, what could you have done for Stefan? He was in one world, and you in another."

The evening before his departure, Olivier stayed a moment with me to drink a cognac in the library. As we didn't know what to talk about, and as a rather embarrassing silence between us dragged on, I got out the photo albums that I had used to entertain Mother years before. My brother commented ironically as he leafed through the pictures. "Only Mother," he said, "could have given a name to that military man in Turkish parade dress, or to that high school student in a uniform with gold buttons and to that adolescent in a peasant costume and the high white lace cap. Is it from a rural branch of our family or the disguise of a child of landed gentry?"

We will never know the answers, I said to myself, and it is too late to ask questions of the elderly lady now a captive of silence forever.

Olivier was struck by the surprising proportion of military men and ecclesiastics in our gallery of ancestors. "The soldiers," he said, "were evidently the sons of a France that kept its eyes glued to the blue line of the Vosges Mountains, and that supposedly thought constantly of Alsace-Lorraine, but never spoke about it (they talked about it all the time, however). The men of the cloth represented all the eche-

148

lons of the hierarchy, from the youthful seminarist to the bishop, while passing through innumerable priests whose cassocks were reinforced by the snug protection of a *cappa magna* or a cope. They wear the black bonds bordered in white no longer found today except in theater costumes of priests. They either stare at the artist photographing them or plunge into the reading of their prayer book. But the photos always breathe the air of the sacristy, that serenity 'engraved with unction' that is given off by the peacefulness of the priesthood, or by the felicitous digestion after a good meal after a baptism or a marriage, when Uncle Canon or Uncle Bishop had been invited to preside."

We noticed, Olivier and I, that we had both forgotten the names of most of these phantoms already turning yellow. I said with a laugh, "We could no longer baptize nine out of ten of our ancestors!" "What are you talking about?" Olivier asked.

I told him that a few months before two visitors had come knocking on the door at Breuil. We had grown accustomed to having traveling salesmen arrive in our parts from all kinds of religious groups—Jehovah's Witnesses, Seventh Day Adventists, and still others. That particular time it was two Frenchmen who had converted to the Church of Jesus Christ of Latter Day Saints. They came to bring us the good word of the Mormons. What most touched me about their religion was the possibility that they made me glimpse of the assurance of the salvation of my ancestors, no matter how separated by generations, if I were to convert to the faith preached by Joseph Smith. A Mormon can actually have his ancestors baptized by simply furnishing their precise civil state to the Church. "The time will come," said the missionary, "when all the baptized will rise again in the glory of Jesus Christ." I felt a bit ashamed when these enlightened youths left us not to be able to tell the names even of my great-grandparents. Our indifference to genealogy condemns our forebears to eternal nothingness, because we have been incapable of baptizing our dead according to the liturgy of the Mormons.

I told Olivier that it is a dogma that seems rather preposterous. But on examination, like all other theological inventions, it surely contains a small kernel of truth in a symbolic way. Those we can still name are retained by that fragile thread, not of life, because they obviously no longer enjoy it, but they are held for an instant in our memories suspended at the edge of the abyss of time where oblivion will swallow up their name.

"You have deep thoughts," said Olivier jokingly (that pleasant tone that permits one to say things in an agreeable way that are not necessarily so agreeable, or whose meaning perplexes the listener).

Olivier looked at Mother's photos. He turned the pages slowly, to the very last pictures where she had become the specter of her former self. Olivier was silent for a moment. I thought he was thinking about Mother. But he said, in a questioning voice:

"I'm probably going to give you a start, Etienne. But I have often wondered just how much you loved our mother. . . . No, I don't mean that you detested her. Right to the end, you conducted yourself toward her in a way . . .

yes, let's not be afraid to use the word, in an *admirable* way. But in your manner of addressing her, of saying, 'Yes, Mother,' with a terrible gentleness, of taking care of her . . . pardon me . . . I often thought that you were taking too much on yourself, that your patience was not at an end, but was almost at an end . . ."

I agreed that that was undoubtedly inevitable with the sick and with disabled elderly people.

"There wasn't only that. You can confess it, you can confess it to yourself. Mother constantly obliged you to live a life that you really didn't want to live . . ."

"Let's not talk any more about that," I said. "Mother was no saint, but she had . . ."

I was almost ashamed to pronounce the word, but then I started again:

"She had a soul."

"I never doubted it," said Olivier. Coldly, as if it were a question of a concrete fact. As if to someone announcing, "The train leaves at nine o'clock," one answers: "I never doubted it."

While Olivier was still there, I did not have the time to ask myself if he was right. He went on to another subject.

"When I learned of Stefan's death, I told myself that you were going to be more alone than ever."

"I'm used to it, you know."

"Stefan really cared for you."

Those were not exactly the words or the tone of voice I would have used. But Olivier went on:

"Two years ago Stefan told me one day: 'You ought to

encourage your brother to write. He has a pen, you know
. . . he has talent.' 'It's you who ought to encourage him,' I
said. Do you know what Stefan answered me?"

"No."

"Etienne is so humble that when I tell him things like
that, I can read in his eyes that he doesn't believe me. He
thinks it's being indulgent or through kindness that I advise
him to write . . . So he needs to admire. He admires me
more than is reasonable, and that doesn't always facilitate
things with him."

"Stefan saw things clearly," I said after a period of silence. "But what he never saw, or at least I hope he didn't,
is that sometimes I . . ."

I didn't finish my sentence. Left up in the air like that,
Olivier was intrigued. I changed the subject. I was not
going to give my brother the satisfaction of confessing that I
could feel jealous of Stefan. I was jealous of his being
elsewhere. As Olivier said: "He was in one world, and you in
another." His world seemed to me to be the real world, the
world of life. Even if he died from it.

I don't stop asking myself questions for which I have no
answer. I tell myself that Stefan did not die of fear, but
rather of stupor or of surprised despair; Laurel and Hardy
had come back. He had gone around the world only to find
them in the same place face to face with him. But when he
took the plane (secretly), was it to go deliberately in search
of death, or perhaps to struggle against "Evil" one final
time? He would have shrugged his shoulders if he had heard
me speak that way. He refused to believe in Evil as an
entity, as a category of one's being. In one of his last

published texts, he had written: "What must be avoided at all cost is the establishment of a coherent philosophy of evil, of finding a single root for evil, and one only, one source and only one, one origin and one only. If evil is born of desire and of concupiscence, men will be condemned to an asceticism that extinguishes desire and greed, but evil will come to life elsewhere. If evil comes from avidity and property, men will be constrained to possess nothing, and evil will be reborn next door, in the power of those who will undertake to forbid possessions for anybody. If evil comes from differences, men will be constrained to resemble one another as perfectly as possible, and those with colored skin or beliefs that aren't identical to the recommended model will be excluded from the city, and evil will be reborn in uniformity. If there are those who profess that evil is the fault of the human heart, they will have said nothing. And if there are those who declare that it's the fault of society, they will not have said anything either. Because what are societies made of? Of men who found societies and are shaped by them, that is, by their very selves. Consequently," Stefan concluded, "all theories of evil cause more evil than the existence of evil itself."

Yes, Stefan refused to believe in Evil-in-itself, but I tell myself more and more frequently that since his death, Evil believes in us. Stefan stood up to Evil. I bend my head before it. What has my life been worth?

I put that question the other day to Vincent, who came back to the country for a couple of days and came over to see me. "You're crazy," he said. He almost got angry. "Don't you know what you've meant to all of us? The way you took care of your parents, and of your mother at the end of her life, of your brother, of your friends. . . . I don't want to use any high-sounding words. . . . But I've always considered you an example . . ."

An example? I still ask myself: an example of what? I'm one of millions of human beings who have been nothing more than spectators en route on the earth. I've observed life from a distance. I had a friend, but he was a friend at a distance.

The fireplace in the library is hard to light. Even with very dry wood, it smokes a while before it really catches. I stupidly stay there shaking the logs with the firetongs, poking at them without a poker. As always, clumsy and useless. The fire catches without me. I got upset for nothing. I simply have tears in my eyes, but without knowing whether it's from sadness or from the smoke.